LOSING GRACELAND

ALSO BY MICAH NATHAN

Gods of Aberdeen

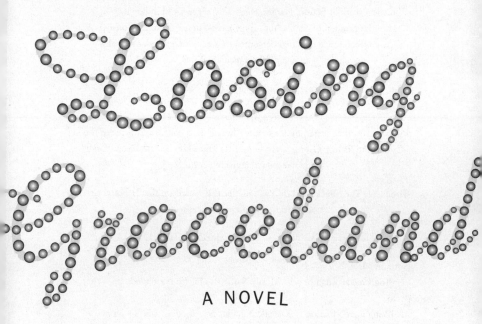

Losing Graceland

A NOVEL

MICAH NATHAN

BROADWAY PAPERBACKS
NEW YORK

This is a work of fiction. Names, characters, places, and incidents either
are the product of the author's imagination or are used fictitiously.
Any resemblance to actual persons, living or dead, events, or locales
is entirely coincidental.

Library of Congress Cataloging-in-Publication Data

Nathan, Micah.
    Losing Graceland: a novel / Micah Nathan.—1st trade pbk. ed.
      p. cm.
    1. Young men—Fiction.   2. College graduates—Fiction.   3. Older men—
Fiction.   4. Presley, Elvis, 1935-1977—Sightings—Fiction.   I. Title.
    PS3614.A86L67 2010
    813'.6—dc22   2010012376

ISBN 978-0-307-59135-7
eISBN 978-0-307-59136-4

Printed in the United States of America

Book design by Maria Elias
Cover design by Nick Castle
Cover photograph by Deborah Schwartz/Getty Images

10 9 8 7 6 5 4 3 2 1

First Edition

For Mom and Dad

Every time I think that I'm getting old, and gradually going to the grave, something else happens.

—*Elvis Presley*

I.

*B*en Fish stood on the front porch of the old man's house and squinted in the morning sun. It was a small brick ranch, three windows with miniblinds and crooked flower boxes set along the front. Across the street children ran and screamed through a sprinkler shaped like a fire hydrant. Ben pushed the doorbell. He took a deep breath. He looked back over his shoulder, at a towheaded child in orange shorts sitting on the neighbor's lawn. The child held his knee and cried while pulsating water soaked his hair and dripped down his arms.

The old man rapped on the inside of his window and spread the miniblinds apart. Ben saw the faint outline of a mouth, and the pads of his fingers pressed to the dusty glass.

"You Ben?" The glass fogged as he spoke.

"Yes, sir."

"Tell me what happened to that boy."

"Pardon?"

"The crying boy. Sitting in the sprinkler. What happened to him."

"I don't know," Ben said. "I think he hurt his knee."

"His knee, huh."

Ben heard the clack of a dead bolt and the door creaked open. He saw the sliver of a dim living room, books stacked waist high. Pools of scattered papers. A brown plaid couch. The edge of a black robe. The man's face stayed hidden behind the door, but his voice was clear and strong, with a whisper of Southern accent. Every word ended softly.

"How's the boy now?"

Ben glanced across the street. The towheaded child laughed, arms held straight overhead, back arched. He screamed with pleasure as he splashed through puddles on the sidewalk.

"He looks okay," Ben said.

"Tough kid. You tough?"

"I guess."

"You guess. Well, that's a big and fast car in my garage. I need someone who can handle big and fast." The old man poked his head around the edge of the door. Half his face stayed hidden in shadow. He narrowed his eye.

Ben fumbled in his creased leather bag and took out a sheet of paper with a photocopy of his license paper-clipped to the corner.

"Driving record?" the man said.

"Yes, sir. I should explain the stop sign—"

A wrinkled hand snatched it from Ben, and he saw the flash of a ring, a wide gold band with a lightning bolt. The door clicked shut. Seconds later it creaked open again. The eye returned.

"Says here you ran a stop sign four years ago."

"That's what I was trying to tell you. I was seventeen."

"That an excuse?"

"Yes."

"Good excuse," the old man said. "Meet me in the garage."

Ben stood by the old man's car. It was a long, low car from the fifties, and it looked like it hadn't been driven since—dull whitewalls, flat tires, pitted chrome runners, and yellowed headlights with glass thick as Coke bottles. Ben peered through the passenger window. He saw cobwebs running from black leather steering wheel to black leather driver's seat. A set of golf clubs sat in the back, dusty irons and woods packed into a leather bag that looked like it would break apart at the first touch.

A push broom leaned against the garage wall, under the light switch, next to a bag of mulch and a garden spade with dried dirt pasted to its blade. The old man ran his hands along the car's hood. Thick dust piled against his fingers. He wore sweatpants and a black terry-cloth robe, brown leather belt cinched around the waist. His shoes were brown leather loafers with tassels. He tossed a key to Ben without looking at him and clapped his hands clean.

"Nineteen fifty-eight Ford Fairlane Skyliner," the old man said. "They don't make this color red anymore."

He had to be an Elvis impersonator, Ben figured. His hair, his mannerisms, the way he talked; it added up to a decrepit version of Elvis, a copy of a copy of a copy, faded and creased, but its source material was unmistakable. And he even looked a little like Elvis, as much as an old, fat Elvis impersonator looks like anything other than an old, fat Elvis impersonator. Puffy cheeks, thick wide nose, joweled chin dusted with baby powder. Thinning hair dyed black as tire rubber, greased into a high wedge, a line of dye ringing his high forehead. He had the hint of an involuntary sneer, a wrinkled curl to his upper lip. Or maybe, Ben thought, he just saw it that way because the sneer was synonymous with Elvis. You couldn't see one without thinking of the other, and you couldn't think of one without seeing the other.

"Colors are made from formulas," the old man continued. "And this cherry red was a secret some sonofabitch scientist took to his grave."

"It's impressive," Ben said.

"Goddamn right it is. Now start her up."

He slid in through the passenger door, smelling old cigarettes and dry leather. The seat creaked. A napped layer of dust blanketed the dashboard. Ketchup packets lay beneath the brake pedal, next to paper cups, fast-food wrappers, and crumpled receipts.

Ben turned the key and nothing happened. He turned it again and looked at the old man through the windshield, shrugging.

The old man pulled his robe closer. "Pop the hood."

He lifted it with a grunt, then stepped back and put his hands on his hips.

"Sonofabitch," the old man said. "I can't remember who I loaned the engine to."

They took Ben's car, a little Honda hatchback that the old man cursed at while he squeezed himself into the seat.

"How much did you pay for this piece of shit?" the old man said.

"Two grand," Ben said.

"In 1962 I paid five for that Fairlane. Take a right on Porter."

The morning sun ricocheted off the Honda's hood and Ben put on his sunglasses, but the old man stared straight into the glare, tapping his fingers on one knee. He'd changed into red sweatpants and a matching red sweatshirt. He still wore his brown loafers. His gold lightning bolt ring glowed.

"You know Sal's?" the old man said.

"I'm not that familiar with this area—"

"Five miles down. Can't miss it. Big old sign says 'Sal's.'"

"What's at Sal's?"

"Something to replace my Fairlane. We got a lot of driving ahead."

Ben saw the ad two days ago, buried in the classifieds under telemarketing jobs and offers for home massages:

DRIVER NEEDED SEVEN DAYS EXCELLENT PAY NO DRUGGIES DRUNKS OR FELONS.

He called the number on a Tuesday night after he'd had a few beers. The old man told him to show up at his address at eight A.M. sharp, and when Ben asked if he should bring anything, the old man said a driving record. How about my résumé, Ben said, and the old man said a man's face is his résumé, then he hung up and left Ben wondering if he should bother.

But he bothered because for the first time in his life he had no other plans. His final semester was over, Jessica had still dumped him, and his options—going back home, or staying in town and working another summer at the Palisade Mall folding ties at Harold's—would lead to an existential crisis. A genuine existential crisis, not like the trust-fund kids who wander Europe, searching for authenticity in hostels. He wouldn't emerge from his summer mall job a better person; he'd emerge defeated, having thrown up his hands at the age of twenty-one. An office job by twenty-three, married with one child by thirty, living in his hometown, feigning interest in lawn mowers and gutter guards, and forever lamenting the missed opportunities of his youth. His midlife crisis would come early, the outcome preordained.

He knew he couldn't live with his mom back home, because remnants of his dead father lay all over the house. His dad's winter wool jacket still hung in the garage. His old sneakers were buried in the front closet, his razor sat in the medicine cabinet, his stained sweatshirt waited on the washing machine, collecting lint and dark globs of spilled laundry detergent. His ghost sat at the kitchen table and listened in on Ben's conversations with his mom. His ghost opened the door to Ben's old room and peered in, before disappearing into shadow and dust.

Sometimes Ben dreamt of his dad, quiet dreams where no one spoke. They just walked, Ben along a dirt road, his father up ahead. Past dark blue forests, their steps marked by the crunch of gravel and the chants of cicadas hidden deep within the brush. He could never catch up and his father never slowed down. The first few times Ben had tried to shout but found his voice lost. Choked and suffocated; no breath for a whisper. In subsequent dreams he learned to only trudge along, looking for evidence of his dad in footprints.

No one had warned him how frustrating grief was. How it lingered long past its welcome, past the first few months when it cleansed like a fast. At first he'd felt special, almost chosen. Not anymore, Ben realized. In the year since his father's death, the grief had gone rotten; he could smell its stink everywhere, like foul meat carried in his pocket.

Ben pulled his Honda into Sal's Used Cars, where hopefuls lined up with balloons whipsawing at the ends of string tied to side-view mirrors and antennas. The old man told Ben to wait in the car. He pulled himself out with a grunt, smoothed back his hair, and tugged at the bottom of his red sweatshirt.

Sal was halfway across the lot before the old man made it to the first row.

"Morning, chief," Sal said, blue tie flapping in the wind. "You ready to sell that Skyliner?"

"No," the old man said, "but I need a car."

Sal eyed the Honda. "Trade-in?"

"Ain't mine."

"Then how about that Skyliner."

"Now listen," the old man said. "If you ask me again—"

Sal waved him off. "I'm just doing what I do, chief. You know I'd kick myself if I didn't ask twice." He flashed his bleached teeth and rubbed the lobe of his plucked ear. "That cherry red gets me hard. Some son of a bitch scientist took the secret to his—"

"I know the story," the old man said. "I'm looking for something big and fast. Low miles. Good AC."

Sal turned on his heels and surveyed his lot with a frown. He repeated "big and fast," over and over.

"How does an 'eighty-six Olds sound?"

The old man shook his head.

"'Ninety-eight Pathfinder?"

"That an SUV?"

Sal nodded.

"I'm driving to Memphis," the old man said. "Not the jungles of Zaire."

"Well, then, I'm afraid all I got left is a 1965 Cadillac El Dorado

Seville. Custom supercharged V8. Wisteria on white, stainless and chrome."

The old man thought for a moment.

"All right, Sal. Let's see the goddamn thing."

He sat in the driver's seat, in the far corner of the lot. Sun had warmed the steering wheel; the leather smelled like summer.

"What's wrong with it?" the old man said.

Sal grinned. "Nothing. Start her up."

He revved the engine. He closed his eyes and revved again. He knew he was in the back lot of a used-car dealer in Cheektowaga, New York—the kind of town where strip malls were mountains and a puddle of sprinkler water on a suburban sidewalk the ocean—but he saw her anyway. A laughing beauty queen sitting next to him, her long legs dangling out the window and the wind caressing her auburn hair. Pink polish on her pink little toes, a glittering anklet, pink shorts hiked up to the top of her smooth tan thighs. She'd been a dancer; a winner of local pageants; a churchgoing girl. When she sang hymns, her perfect little mouth turned into a tight O and her red lipstick looked like the color of fresh roses after a spring rain. She squeezed his arm and he pressed the pedal, head thrown back, howling.

Back when I rambled, he thought. A rambler roaring through the world, drinking oceans dry and chopping down mountains.

"Hey, chief. Watch the RPMs."

The old man opened his eyes. He took a deep breath, staring at his hands still gripping the steering wheel. Wrinkled hands the color of sand patched with wet spots. Hands that had once dipped into the primordial ooze and brought up life leaking from between his fingers, running down his arm, dripping onto his shoes. Life everyone wanted. They'd kill for a teaspoon of that muck. A fistful of that ooze.

"Now, is she a beauty, or is she a beauty," Sal said.

"The most beautiful thing I ever seen," the old man said, and he wiped the tears from his cheeks and reached for his wallet.

2.

MEMPHIS, Tennessee—Nadine Emma Brown, the long-rumored illegitimate granddaughter of Elvis Presley, was reported missing last week from the Taste O' Sugar gentleman's club, where Ms. Brown worked as an exotic dancer. In an exclusive DAILY DISH interview, a source close to Ms. Brown revealed that Ms. Brown had possible connections to the Memphis underworld. . . .

*Y*ou finished?"
Ben nodded, and the old man folded the magazine clipping, delicately slipping it back into a coffee-ring-stained manila envelope. Then he asked the waitress for another vanilla Coke and took a few bites of his apple pie.

They sat in an imitation 1950s diner, in a cracked red booth against a wall marked with penciled graffiti and dried spots of food. The 1965 Cadillac El Dorado Seville waited outside the front window. Ben watched a steady string of cars zip down the boulevard, stragglers from the morning commute.

He thought about his meeting last month with the college career adviser, a portly middle-aged man wearing a faded pin-stripe shirt stretched to its limits. He'd taken one perfunctory look at Ben's transcript and asked him what sort of career he wanted.

"I don't know," Ben said.

"Well, you majored in anthropology. What about graduate school."

"I'm not ready for a career," Ben said. "I want to travel, maybe live in Amsterdam for a while."

"In an anthropological context?"

"What?"

"Isn't that what anthropologists do? Live in different cultures, take notes . . ."

"Yeah, but I don't want to be an anthropologist. I just want to hang out."

The adviser leaned forward, his chair creaking in protest. "Son, if you don't want to be an anthropologist, then why did you major in anthropology?"

Ben shrugged. "I liked the professors."

The waitress set down the vanilla Coke and the old man smiled at her. She blossomed red and walked away, looking over her shoulder, but the old man was focused on Ben.

"I cut that article from a gossip rag," the old man said. "And I've been holding on to it for the past month, trying to figure if it's true or not. Now, a gossip rag is a gossip rag, and most of what they print I wouldn't waste on a broke-dick dog. But I always knew I had a granddaughter that never knew me."

"Nadine," Ben said.

The old man sipped his Coke and crunched an ice cube. "That's right. Until last month I thought the days were punishment. Then I was standing in line at the store and on the magazine rack I saw that headline"—he patted the manila envelope—"and I realized that sometimes the days are gods. They bless us with opportunities for redemption, even if we don't deserve them. *Especially* if we don't deserve them. Which brings us to now."

Ben looked down at his cheeseburger, half eaten with a glob of ketchup squirted out the side.

"I'll pay you ten thousand to drive me to Memphis," the old man said. "I'd drive myself, but my eyes aren't what they were, and we can't take the highways because everyone goes too goddamn fast. We can't afford an accident. You understand?"

"Ten *thousand*?"

"Five thousand now, five thousand when we get there. Cash. However you want it. Twenties, fifties, hundreds. Nickels, dimes, quarters. In a sack or lined up in a briefcase. I'll cover all expenses—food, drink, hotel. But we won't be stopping much because we don't have the time. If something happened to Nadine, we need to get down there quick before the trail grows cold. If I had to guess, I'd say she got herself mixed up with some amateur gunslinger, some low-rent thug looking for young tail and no commitments. Probably had her dealing drugs on the side, pushing profits to him. I been leaned on pretty goddamn hard by those sons of bitches. Back when I didn't know any better. Back when low-rent thugs looked like high-rent rollers."

"Ten thousand is a lot of money," Ben said.

The old man nodded. "Goddamn right it is. What's the point of money if you can't use it for something noble? Something better than fancy sunglasses and ruby rings? Something more than a gold medallion with a sapphire Jewish star . . . what's it called? You know what I'm talking about, man. The Jewish star. What's it called."

"Star of David?"

"That's right." The old man snapped his fingers. "You Jewish?"

"My father was Jewish."

"What does that make you?"

"Confused."

The old man nodded again. "I've spent enough money to make Solomon puke. Wasted it on phonies and frauds, con men and cocksuckers looking for a teaspoon of the muck. And at the end of the day—"

He stopped suddenly, pinching the bridge of his nose. He shut his eyes and Ben thought he was going to sneeze. Then the old man choked back a sob, and Ben looked around for the waitress to bring him something. A cup of coffee, a hug from a pretty lady, whatever it would take . . .

"All I'm saying," the old man said through a clot of mucus that rattled when he cleared his throat. He opened his eyes. "All I'm saying is the money don't mean a thing."

Ben waited as the old man blew his nose into his napkin.

"Ten thousand is a lot of money," Ben repeated.

The old man sniffled. "Maybe for you."

"But you can fly to Memphis, first class, for a tenth of what you'd pay me to drive. And if time is important—"

The old man brought his fist down on the table and their glasses rattled. People turned and stared. His upper lip quivered as he spoke. "Son, do you think I'd put my fate and Nadine's into the hands of some pilot?"

"I don't—"

"I remember those two fools they pulled off that Boeing 737. Saw it on CNN. They were hopped up on weed and God knows what else. Levorphanol, from the looks of it. Even in the goddamn press conference, when the one with that Clark Kent hair went on about how sorry he was. Christ, he was hopped up then. And even if you get past the pilots, you still got to worry about a hijacking. You can't tell me they put U.S. Marshals on every goddamn plane. X-ray machines and metal detectors don't always work. Not with the polymers they use now, and the ceramics, and who the hell knows what else."

Ben looked out the diner window, across the wide boulevard, to the rows of apartment buildings with parking lots for front lawns. He wanted to give the impression he was thinking it over. Ten grand would solve his problems. Get an apartment in Amsterdam, live like a bohemian. He wouldn't need much—a bicycle, decent food, a couple cases of cheap wine, and enough spare cash for the occasional date. Ten grand would give him escape. A white board with fresh markers that he could use to draw whatever history he wanted.

Escape, he realized. The town, the mall, his apartment suddenly became a locked room with cement-gray bars surrounded by the thrum of traffic and the plastic smell of . . . what? Conformity was too easy a label, mediocrity too elitist. It was something else. Disappointment, maybe. Or tacit acceptance.

Ben stared at the old man. A black lock of hair fell down over his forehead and for a moment he really looked like Elvis. Not that Ben knew what Elvis really looked like—he only knew him from diner clocks and the silly beach movies he'd watched as a kid. But whoever that Elvis was, the old man looked just like him.

"Is this a serious offer?" Ben said.

"Serious as cancer."

"Ten thousand for me to drive you to Memphis. That's all I have to do."

"That's all."

"Can I ask you a personal question?"

The old man sat back and took a swig of vanilla Coke. He crunched an ice cube. "Shoot."

"Who are you?"

"It's not who I am, but who I was."

"Then who were you."

The old man swallowed the shards of ice. He smoothed back his hair and his eyes dropped half lid. Heavy eyes, thick lids, dark bags beneath like halved grapes.

"I was the King."

Their apartment sat above Manchurian House, a Chinese restaurant off the wide boulevard surrounded by treeless flat and the crenellated horizon of low-slung strip malls and plazas. A framed poster of Brando hung above the brick fireplace. Ben's roommate, Patrick, sat on a three-legged Naugahyde chair, Ben across from him on the couch. An aquarium stood in the corner, green with algae, two fish swimming blind through the murky water. Home theater speakers hung on the walls.

"He didn't come out and say it," Ben said. "He didn't actually *say* he was Elvis."

Patrick licked his joint closed, spitting a fleck off his lip. He wore jeans and a wrinkled T-shirt, one leg draped over the chair's arm. He wheeled the lighter. "I doubt he even has the ten grand."

"He's got the money," Ben said. "I watched him buy a classic Caddy with a roll of hundreds."

"That was probably his entire stash. Last of the Social Security."

"It wasn't like that."

"Uh-huh. What was it like?"

"I don't know. I haven't figured it out yet."

Patrick exhaled smoke rings. "It sounds kooky." He laughed. "That's a good word. *Kooky*." Another puff, and he shrugged. "You know, you could work with me at city camp. The pay sucks but there's always a few available high school seniors—"

"No thanks."

Patrick grinned. "My bad. I forgot about Jess."

"Don't talk about her."

"Still?"

"Yes. Still."

"Jesus, Ben. It's been almost a year."

"Six months."

"A year. Six months." Patrick puffed, and spoke with his breath held. "Whatever. You need to move the fuck *on*. I'll get you a job at camp, you'll meet a young blonde, and all the pain will just fade . . . away."

Patrick held out the joint but Ben ignored him. Instead he lay back on the couch and put his arm over his face. He remembered how his dad would stomp into the living room fresh from shoveling snow, and the entire house smelled like winter coming off his clothes. Those central New York winters: silent, sharp, and brittle. In the spring his dad smelled of lingering rain. In the summer, warm wind. In the autumn, dry leaves and someone's fireplace. His dad a god who carried the seasons in his pocket, big as the world.

3.

been up all night," the old man said. "Mapping our route. Load these bags into the trunk and I'll be out in a minute." Ben did as the old man said and waited in the driver's seat of the old Cadillac El Dorado, staring into the dark of the garage door. In his bag he'd packed several paperback biographies of Elvis, remainders bought from a sales rack in Barnes & Noble the night before, sandwiched on the shelf between *The 50 Worst Album Covers of All Time* and a book on the Knights Templar. The old man had wanted him at the house by six A.M., and when he showed up on the front step, the old man answered the door wearing his red sweatsuit, holding a muffin in one hand and an electric razor in the other. He was barefoot and gray stubble dotted his puffy face. When he spoke he scratched his head and looked at the ground as though it were speaking to him and he was trying to hear what it had to say.

He'd led Ben into his living room, where maps were spread on the floor next to packed bags, stacks of books, and magazines. The magazines were the type that Ben liked to browse while waiting in line at the drugstore—tales of Nostradamus, Bigfoot, alien abductions, and the occasional Elvis story. Grainy doctored photos of a fat guy in a white jumpsuit peeking out from a car or walking into a gas station restroom, and damn if the old man didn't look a lot like the grainy doctored photos.

"There will be many things you question during our journey together." The old man handed his bag to Ben. "You will question my purpose, my morals, and my lucidity. But always remember that though these old eyes look cloudy, they've seen to the end of the universe. They've peeked through the keyhole in God's bathroom door, gone through the devil's drawers and found his unpaid parking tickets. Now, you don't have to believe me just yet—if I was standing where you're standing, I'd wonder why isn't this crazy fool in a strait-jacket with a stick between his teeth. But until you believe me, pretend to believe me and we'll get on just fine. You eat breakfast?"

Ben nodded.

"Any good?"

"It was okay."

"What was it?"

"A chicken burrito."

"Goddamn, that's a strange breakfast. We'll grab some proper food on the road."

Ben stared into the dark of the garage door and wondered if Patrick was right. Maybe he'd lost his fucking mind. Driving to Memphis with an insane old man in search of a missing strip-per. Face-to-face with the star of tabloid mags and conspiracy theorists, the once-dead king of American kitsch found alive in Cheektowaga, New York. Complete with matching sweatsuit, poorly dyed hair, and a fat gold ring with a lightning bolt.

He remembered his last summer job. One year ago, right after his dad died. Harold's Department Store in the Palisade Mall. He'd taken it in the vain hope of saving enough money for his trip to Amsterdam. That dream sustained him for three months. Any longer and he was worried he'd start humping the mannequins, or eating the bizarre food they sold in the aisles—chocolates in giant gold tins, pickled peppers stuffed into gift-wrapped jars, Swedish fruit bread decorated with red ribbons. He folded ties and flirted with the girls at the makeup counter. Eighties Muzak constantly oozed from ceiling speakers, horn instrumentals of "Papa Don't Preach" and "Maniac."

Sometimes he'd get pot from Patrick and sit in the bathroom at work, toking with a can of Glade in his suit jacket pocket. He felt older than anyone his age, an ancient twenty. He'd left little poems for a girl with long curly brown hair who worked the fragrance counter. Haikus on the back of discarded receipts. *Drinks later at bar/You order something funny/Slippery nipple?*

One day she was fired for stealing perfume gift sets, and Ben watched her being escorted through the aisles, flanked by two security guards, clutching her purse as mascara-stained tears streamed down her blushed cheeks.

He quit and tried living at home, but it was a disaster. He heard his mom talking with his dad's ghost while doing dishes, heard her greet him when she came home. He believed she was going crazy. Really crazy, not just throwing-yourself-at-the-coffin crazy (which she hadn't done, instead doing something scarier like sitting stiff as a board in the front pew and staring ahead while everyone else dabbed their eyes).

The passenger door creaked open. The old man dropped a sack onto Ben's lap. A jumble of hundreds rolled tight, wrapped in rubber bands.

"You didn't look like the briefcase type," the old man said. "Hope you don't mind."

They drove until noon through the hills of southern New York State, a wisteria-on-white speck beneath a giant sky banded with feathered clouds, and they stopped for lunch in a small town just south of Erie, Pennsylvania, that laid claim to the first public library in the country. The restaurant called itself Italian and it served butter-soaked garlic bread in a plastic basket. The old man ordered an iced tea and chicken parm, and Ben decided he couldn't wait any longer.

"There're some things I need to know," Ben said.

The old man wiped butter off his chin. He'd changed at the first rest stop into a white sweatsuit with a black belt, gold lion's head buckle askew because the duct tape no longer held it tight to the leather.

"Shoot," the old man said.

"Have you contacted the police about your granddaughter?"

The old man leaned forward. "Now, why would I go and do something stupid like that?"

"Because it's their job. Finding missing people."

"Police find bodies," the old man said, "not people."

"That's a nice outfit," the waitress said. She set down the iced tea and took a straw from behind her ear, pausing with it in midair. Her black hair showed white roots. She stood with one hand on her waist. She looked at Ben, then back at the old man.

"This your grandson?"

"I'm his driver," Ben said.

The waitress raised an eyebrow. "A driver? You must be rich."

"Just blind," the old man said.

"Oh, I doubt that." She sauntered away, straw still in hand.

The old man winked at Ben. He drank his iced tea.

"Are you hiding from the law?" Ben said.

"I'm a fugitive. But I'm no criminal."

"I don't understand."

"I'm not paying you to understand. I'm paying you to drive."

"Fair enough," Ben said. "But if something happens and the police pull us over—"

"Obey the traffic laws and we won't have to worry."

"I'm just saying things happen sometimes. And if they do—"

"If they do, you keep your mouth shut and let me handle it."

Ben rubbed his forehead. "Can I ask you another question?"

"Might as well."

"Where were you born?"

"Tupelo. Jesus, who doesn't know that."

"What was your first public performance?"

"Professional or amateur."

"Amateur."

The old man narrowed his eyes in thought. "Mississippi Alabama Fair. If you want to get technical, one year earlier I auditioned for the role of Johnny Appleseed in the school play. Had to sing for it. Didn't get the part."

"What year did you get your first guitar?"

The old man sipped his iced tea. "Is this a fucking quiz?"

"I'm just curious."

"I don't have to prove myself to nobody. Especially you. Now, if this is how it's gonna be—"

"It isn't."

The old man sipped again. "You're one tightly wound sonofabitch. Anyone ever tell you that?"

"Not in those exact words, but yes. All the time."

"You need one of those spiritual retreats," the old man said. "Take a year off in India or something—get yourself a robe, a bowl of rice, and let the universe decide what you're made for. It'll do it, too. The universe is always saying something good."

"What did it say to you?"

"Nothing. Already knew I'd be who I was. But a year in India would've been nice. I'd stay at one of those places where the gurus hang . . . what the hell they called . . ."

"Ashrams," Ben said.

The old man snapped his fingers. "That's right. I don't care for those Indian girls, though. Big noses and little mustaches."

When the waitress returned, the old man pulled her aside. He took out a thick roll of hundreds and closed her hand around the roll of money.

"You got some folks who eat here and can't afford the good stuff," the old man said. "The steak and veal, I mean. Maybe even a glass of wine. Am I right?"

The waitress stared at the money held in her fist, at the old man's mottled hand wrapped around her own.

"I guess," she said.

"Fact is, same old same old drives even a good man to addiction. Drugs, pornography, gambling. A five-dollar pasta platter, week after week, turns them away from hope. I don't imagine the owner is the generous sort, willing to cut a good man a deal. Give that good man a steak instead of a burger. Veal cutlets instead of spaghetti. Am I right?"

"He hasn't given me a raise in two years," the waitress said.

"You take this money, then," the old man said. "Keep a couple hundred for yourself. Use the rest to help some of them good men who can't afford better. Buy his family a couple steaks. Ice cream sundaes for his kids. A bottle of wine for his wife. Make him feel *important*."

"Are you serious?" she said.

"Do I look serious?"

"I can't tell."

"Darling, this is my serious face."

The waitress frowned. "What am I supposed to do? Ask every family who comes in here if they can't afford a better meal?"

"You look like a smart lady," the old man said. "Figure it out."

The waitress glanced at Ben, and he nodded as if to say, *Yeah, I know.*

After lunch they walked past the town hall, a brick building with white columns, and the lampposts were all ornate black iron that looked incongruous on sidewalks next to franchise sub shops, a video store, and a hair salon with faded fashion magazine photos plastered inside the glass. The sun glowed pale behind a gang of thick clouds and Ben had heard on the restaurant radio there was rain where they were headed. South to Cleveland. Another three hours by way of side streets, backways, and small towns with twenty-mile-per-hour speed limits.

The old man said he needed to walk because his back was tight from sitting in the car. The chicken he'd ordered wasn't just not agreeing with him; the way he figured, it was engaged in a full-scale war with his lower intestine.

They walked to the end of Main Street and doubled back, the old man rubbing his stomach, belching and wincing, like he was a veteran of many gastrointestinal wars and knew the right balance of attack and retreat. When they got back to their car, the old man stopped and leaned his arms on the roof, gazing out over the town hall lawn.

"What I'm about to tell you will sound like the biggest pile of horse shit you ever heard," the old man said. "You won't hear this story anywhere else. Not from any book or documentary."

Ben kicked at a pebble and watched it skitter across the street.

"But you have to swear that what I'm going to tell you remains between us and God," the old man said.

"I swear."

"I mean really swear. Not the kind of swear where you tell your woman and make her swear, and she tells her friends and they all swear."

"I really swear," Ben said, "and you don't need to worry because I don't have a girlfriend."

"Why not?"

"I got dumped."

"How long ago?"

"Six months and eight days."

The old man belched again. "You been laid since?"

"No."

"We'll fix that. Best medicine, another woman. Hair of the goddamn dog."

The old man put his hands on his lower back and leaned backward. Ben heard a drumroll of cracks. The old man sighed. Then he told his tale, and it was, as he said, the biggest pile of horse shit Ben had ever heard.

The Old Man's Tale

By 1977 I'd had enough. Shit my pants in Indianapolis after "Early Morning Rain," and by the time I stumbled off the stage, the shit had drained into my shoe and I was walking around with a shoeful of shit, smelling terrible, and Schilling says to one of the roadies, *You keep farting like that and I'll shove a cork up your ass.* Course, we both knew it was me—I'd shit myself in Rapid City five days earlier—but Schilling wanted me to save face. He was good like that.

I was in a bad place, doing bad things. Everyone knew it, but no one asked me to stop. People said you can't help a man who won't be helped; no such thing, a man who won't be helped. He just needs someone to hold his hand until he's ready for salvation. Ginger said something about rehab. I told her she was fucking nuts. No difference between rehab and a show, I told her. Flashbulb entrance, band intro, some ballads, and the big finish; no difference at all. The minute I'd have checked out of rehab there'd be a bucket of pills waiting in the limo and a six-week contract in Vegas. No one cared, man. I was a golden calf squirting bullion from my tits, and everyone lined up with their mouths open.

The official report says I died on August 16, 1977. But in truth I died the day I began to hate, and I'd been hating for as long as I could remember. I hated the goddamn fans who didn't care if I forgot the words, I hated the goddamn cameras that kept looking for someone handsome when all I had was ugly. I hated the goddamn women who were looking to be my Mary, talking about *You're the sweetest man I ever knew* when everyone around me knew I wasn't sweet. If I could've put a bullet between the eyes of every sonofabitch that screamed themselves hoarse whenever I faked my way through "Polk Salad Annie," you'd be looking at a man who gave the Angel of Death a run for his money.

Five million in 1977 goes a long way, and here's what it got me: peace. Kept the circle tight, made sure everyone got paid, and let everyone else believe what I wanted them to. It didn't take much, and it wasn't as hard as I thought it'd be. I'd been giving people what they wanted for twenty years. Pretending Elvis was alive was a hell of a lot harder than pretending he's dead.

"So that's it," Ben said.

"That's it. What do you think."

Ben looked over his shoulder, across the street. Their waitress had taken a cigarette break and she stood on the sidewalk in front of the restaurant. One hand on her hip, cigarette between two fingers. She stared at them.

Yeah, Ben thought. I know.

"I think ten thousand is a lot of money," Ben said.

The old man sighed and looked skyward. "Looks like rain. We better get rambling."

4.

One year earlier a young woman talking on her cell phone jumped the curb and plowed Ben's father into a hot dog cart. His father had been having lunch with his coworker June, and she broke her collarbone, pelvis, and suffered third-degree burns when french fry grease splattered across her legs. He died instantly, though Ben wondered how the coroner knew that. He just figured it was something they told family members to make them feel better, but he hoped his father had held on for as long as he could, so he could prepare himself for death and not be snuffed out like an ant crushed under a shoe.

Death by hot dog stand made it performance art. Ben realized this—the lethal hot dog cart was now part of his family narrative, a tragic tale that lacked the irony to reach surreal. If only his father had heart disease, and if only his doctor had warned him the week before that his penchant for greasy hot dogs would be the death of him . . . but it was too much to ask. The universe doesn't believe in compensation; its better narratives are accidental, and Ben was left with the image of his father lying in a bloody jumble next to a stainless-steel hot dog cart, *Kosher Franks* yellow umbrella tilting on the sidewalk like a scene from a French movie.

The funeral was common, the cards were plentiful and heartfelt, and the world gave him and his mom a wide berth. Everyone seemed to talk in whispers. Everything was in bright focus. Giddiness. Despair. Floating through class, through campus, through the mall. Self-absorption run wild. Department store songs a message of healing. His dad's ghost in a stranger's smile. Apophenia, it's called. Finding meaning in meaningless events, seeing patterns in random data.

The old man slept, snoring quietly, his head bobbing with every bump and pothole. Ben gazed at the road and remembered his first girlfriend. Molly Howe in sixth grade. He'd given her a Valentine's card with a little candy heart that read *Will U B Mine?* The next day she brought him a sugar cookie wrapped in a pink bow, and they shared it over lunch in the cafeteria. She seemed nervous, fidgety, laughing too hard at his jokes. He was self-aware even then, he realized, incapable of enjoying the simple pleasures of a sixth-grade girlfriend.

She laughed and he remembered seeing a speck of sugar cookie stuck to her cheek. She laughed again, brown mush between her teeth. They'd had hot dogs for lunch with skinny french fries, and that sugar cookie wrapped in a pink bow for dessert. He remembered at that moment he didn't want to be her boyfriend anymore. He remembered she disgusted him.

As the sun set, the old man awoke and asked where they were. He hated sleep. Always had. Saw it as a scrimmage for dying, because it came and you had no control over it, and then it showed nothing but nightmares and fire. Whispers from the grave, the same whispers the old man figured all old men heard. Whispers of regret and guilt. No more chances. All used up.

And the books. Goddammit, the books. They all spoke hogwash—life after death, reincarnation, transmigration and transmogrification. Would his soul occupy a tree somewhere in Tupelo? Or a dandelion in Cheektowaga? Would he be reborn into a baby in India? Or would he just lie in the ground and rot?

Please no, he thought. Let me become a handsome young man on the beach. Sand between my toes and stomach fluttery from watching pretty little things walk by. Something good when I look in the mirror. Thick hair, tight skin, bronzed and beautiful; I'll take that life at thirty. Forty, even. Hell, I'll take it at fifty if that's the best you can do.

The old man figured even if there was a God he'd already forsaken His gift of life, so there may as well be nothing. He couldn't say for certain what had happened to him—some nights he woke up gasping for air, covered in sweat, and he couldn't remember his life. Maybe it was all fantasy, shoveling myth into the sinkholes riddling his age-addled mind. Maybe the hazy memories were hazy for a reason. Charlie Hodge had told him stories about his father, a victim of Alzheimer's. How he claimed he'd fought in the Battle of Ieper in WWI when he'd actually been a cobbler on the Jersey Shore, deemed unfit for military service due to scoliosis.

Jesus Fucking Christ, the old man thought he remembered saying. Charlie, swear if that ever happens to me, you'll put one between my eyes.

Charlie promised but the old man knew they all made a lot of promises back then. When the world was their giant fried oyster. Before the great big lie. The whopper to end all whoppers. So big he'd abandoned everyone and everything he knew. I must have needed it so bad, he thought, that I was willing to trade death for a life without my daughter. It must have been worse than I remember. If I remember.

The map lay in Ben's lap. The old man had traced the route with a red marker. The road rose and dipped, a narrow strip with a dirt shoulder and weeds on either side. Small homes set atop small lawns with garden sculptures of bent-over hausfraus in polka-dot underwear. The evening sky was hemmed in by overhanging trees.

It was Monday and Ben thought about last Monday's basketball game at the town park with Jim and Steve. Jim wore his favorite basketball shirt, picture of a jacked guy dunking on a hundred-foot rim. Samantha watched like she always did, feigning disinterest, gabbing on her cell and smoking her little black cigarettes, a bad habit she'd picked up last semester in Paris. One semester abroad and she came back a Francophile, and Steve figured she'd fucked some Frenchman but he was willing to let it slide because he said the thought of it kind of turned him on. Besides, Steve had said, I haven't been one hundred percent faithful anyway. I slept with this girl at work. A little Asian hottie. I don't know what it is about Cheesecake Factory, but they hire the hottest chicks.

I can't believe you cheated on Samantha, said Ben, and Steve grinned, waving to Samantha, who sat behind the pole at the end of the court, Indian-style, with a cellphone pressed to one ear, a thin trail of smoke rising from the little black cigarette pinched between her thumb and forefinger.

Cheating on a hot girl sends the world a message, Steve said. Like you can trash a Ferrari because you got three others waiting in the garage.

Ben thought about Carrie, the one girl he'd cheated on Jessica with. Had Carrie been a Ferrari? No—she was more like a customized Hyundai, if Hyundais had any sort of edgy appeal.

Passing headlights lit the old man's eyes. "Where are we?" he asked.

"Near Ashland," Ben said.

"Where's Ashland?"

"Ohio."

"You been driving long?"

"Four hours."

"I had a dream." The old man rubbed his face. "Saw myself lying in my grave and the preacher was laughing."

Ben thought about Jessica. Two months before the end. Before she left for college and made him regret every moment he'd spent with her, cursed every time he'd deluded himself into believing they'd be together forever like some ridiculous young couple in a fifties movie. For fuck's sake, she was a virgin before they met— did he seriously think she'd stay with him? That they'd get *married*?

Yes. And he knew it made him sound like a douche bag, but he couldn't help it. He'd never had a girlfriend that hot. He considered himself average in every respect. Average height, average looks, average straight brown hair. With Jessica he felt like the star of his own movie. Like everyone was watching. Watching her sleep in his bed when the lights were low, candle reflection glowing softly on the baby fat of her cheeks.

It had been a big deal the first time Jessica spent the night at his apartment. She'd lied to her parents and told them she was going camping with her best friend, Mindy. Ben bought candles and put on some Miles Davis, bought a framed Brando poster for the living room and a Klimt poster for his room, bought goat cheese, and crackers made from organic wheat, dusted with French sea salt.

She arrived with an overnight bag. Frayed cutoff shorts, tight plum-colored tank, blond hair in a ponytail. Lips glistening, eyes bright and wet. Patrick flirted with her a little, and she flirted back in the way all high school girls flirt with college guys. Ben finally corralled her into his room. She ate some cheese and told him she hated jazz. They talked for hours. He couldn't remember what they talked about. Any discussion of high school was taboo. They ran out of things to say, then fucked, and when they finished Ben sat up and stared at her. She told him to stop staring. He asked why and she said, Because it's weird.

Jessica woke around seven A.M. She kept asking if he thought her mom knew she'd lied. She complained she didn't smell like a campfire because everyone smells like a campfire after a night of camping. She fell into an immature bad mood, the high-school-girl pout, the unwillingness to relax and take a few puffs or fuck until you felt better. Her childish anger seemed to Ben a vestigial limb.

He dropped her off at Mindy's. A peck on the lips, then Ben shuddered as he watched Jessica sprint up Mindy's driveway. He drove back and crashed on the couch, waking up to Patrick taking hits from his three-liter Coke bong. They ate lunch in their grungy kitchen, sitting at a table covered in dirty dishes and pizza boxes.

Patrick cracked the end of a chicken wing and munched on the charred marrow. He smiled at Ben.

You two had fun last night?

We did, Ben said. Many times.

A blonde with small feet and big tits, Patrick said. How did you ever land someone like her?

Ben glared, and Patrick laughed.

Are you *angry*? For real?

Ben said nothing.

Bet you she can suck her own nipples. Does she suck her own nipples?

He shoved Patrick. The box of wings toppled, bones spilling. Patrick shoved Ben back, half smiling. They grappled and rolled into the living room, and it ended when Ben punched Patrick in the mouth, his lip parting like a wet paper towel. Blood poured down the front of Patrick's shirt, onto his jeans, onto the brown carpet.

What the uck? Patrick had screamed. *Asshole. Ucking asshole.*

"Stop at the first bar you see," the old man said. "I'm in the mood for something fried."

Ben had called Jessica from the hospital. She was taking a day trip to Toronto because she'd applied to college at UT.

Why not University of Buffalo? Ben had asked her.

We can't go to the same college, Jessica had said. It would be like we're married.

He said nothing because he knew Jessica was on loan. She was far too beautiful to be anything other than a high-end lease. For the first three months he'd had the upper hand by virtue of being a college guy with an apartment, messy hair, clear skin, and a sob story about his father's tragic death. But then one night he'd had an awful realization, remembering how he viewed the college guys who dated the hot girls in his high school.

Losers. Losers who couldn't get birds their own age, so they had to dip down. And even the hot high-school girls knew it, but they were so eager to play grown-up—to drink bad wine, eat bad cheese, and engage in angst-ridden late-night group talks while lounging on papasans—that they bided their time until they learned how to give proper head.

Losers, Ben thought, and the next five months he never forgot. The first time Jessica swallowed, he realized it was already happening. The next week she grabbed her giant breasts while riding him, and stared at him with wide brown eyes as if to say, *Teach me what else to do so I can please my future boyfriends.*

He remembered driving Patrick home from the hospital. It was a quiet, sullen ride, Patrick with a Darvocet prescription and ten stitches in his lip. Patrick dry-swallowed three pills and Ben helped him up the stairs. Then Jessica called and said she wasn't going to Toronto. Why don't they go to the mall instead. Her mom hadn't suspected a thing.

They ate in the food court. Red plastic trays and screaming children. Ben bought Jessica two bagfuls of clothing, and stood by like a silent idiot when she ran into a gaggle of high-school friends and showed them her new outfits.

"There," the old man said. "Pull over there."

The bar was called Sensations, a cinder-block box with a buzzing neon sign that advertised *Karaoke Night Ladies Drink FREE!* It had a pool table and a dark bar with a gleaming brass footrest. Bikers mingled with locals in Carhart jackets, but there were a few suburban types who drank more than anyone else, husbands in high-waisted jeans and wives in low-cut blouses showing cleavage that rivaled any biker chick. The old man and Ben took a corner booth, and the old man ordered fried shrimp with a pitcher of beer.

Ben tried to ignore the stares. Men at the bar looked over their shoulders. Suburban couples whispered.

"If you're in hiding, you sure don't dress like it," Ben said.

The old man munched a fried shrimp and washed down the grease with a swig of beer. "I'm not in hiding."

Ben grabbed a shrimp. "But you said you were a fugitive."

"No one believes I'm alive. No family to speak of. No friends, no lovers. I could jump up right now and tell everyone who I am, and they'd laugh."

"So why do you dress like that?"

The old man tossed a tail onto his plate. "Like what."

"Like a trailer-park Elvis."

The old man licked his fingers. "You been waiting to use that line or did you just come up with it right now?"

"It's not a line. I'm trying to understand."

"I dress how I want to dress." The old man poured the rest of the pitcher into his glass. "I'm the freest man in the world. Freer than you. How would you dress if you could dress the way you wanted? And don't tell me you'd wear jeans and a T-shirt, because that's bullshit. You'd walk around in your bathrobe, maybe just your underwear and a pair of comfortable socks. Maybe even turn your socks inside out 'cause that way the seams don't itch."

The old man pointed at his lion's head belt buckle. "You see this here? Had it custom-made in Spoke, Alabama. Melted gold from the fillings of a Confederate general. Made in a shop owned by a little Chinese woman who'd married a Navy man. They'd seen my show in Birmingham and told me if I was ever in the neighborhood to come on by and they'd make something for me. The lion head is a Chinese guardian dog. They call it *Shi*."

A woman with high blond hair stepped onto the little stage in the corner of the room and announced that the karaoke contest was beginning. Someone shouted, "Show us your tits," and there was scattered laughter and she wiggled her chest, giving an exaggerated wink like a Kabuki actor.

Then she stepped off the stage and a man in his mid-forties with wrinkle-free khakis and a short-sleeve button-down grabbed the mike off the PA and belched into it. "Ladies and gentlemen, I'd like to kick things off with an oldie but a goodie," he said, and he pointed to the short bald man operating the karaoke machine.

Expectant silence and then he wailed the opening lines of "Jailhouse Rock." The crowd applauded as he performed a decent imitation, complete with creaky hip swivels, spastic leg, and limp wrist. Ben shot a look at the old man, who drank his beer and plucked the last of the crispy bits off his shrimp plate.

"Well?" Ben said.

The old man wrinkled his high forehead. "Well what."

"How's he doing?"

"Terrible. They're always terrible."

The wrinkle-free khaki man finished with another belch and was replaced by a youngish red-haired woman crooning "Love Me Tender." The next man got halfway through "Suspicious Minds," then asked if he could switch to "Treat Me Like a Fool," but the crowd turned him down with boos and catcalls. One of the bikers gulped a shot before leaving his table, and he strutted onto stage while his brethren whooped and hollered, and he ripped off a savage rendition of "Lawdy Miss Clawdy" that brought the house down. When he finished he strode off the stage. One of the suburban husbands gave him a high five. He slapped the husband's hand and grabbed his wife, picking her up off her feet, and she squealed and kicked her high heels while the husband forced a laugh and patted him on the back of his leather jacket.

"You should get up there," Ben said.

The old man ignored him and sucked the crumbs off a shrimp tail. The blond woman with high hair stepped back onto the stage.

One of the bikers looked over at the old man and hollered, "What about him?" Everyone turned to stare. The old man held up his hand, shaking his head.

Glasses rattled and the blond woman onstage whistled into the microphone. The wrinkle-free khaki man began to chant, *"El-vis, El-vis."* Soon the entire bar chanted, stomping their feet, banging their beer mugs on the tables.

"Get up there," Ben said. "You said no one would believe you anyway."

The old man looked down. "I know what I said, goddammit."

The old man smoothed back his hair and stood. His hip hurt. He scanned the room: openmouthed faces, alcohol-reddened eyes, and French manicures. An Elvis clock sat above the bar, man-child in a slim dark suit with his arms the hours and minutes.

He began his march through the crowd, hands pressing against his white sweatsuit, fingers clutching at the lion's head belt buckle. The duct tape finally gave, and it clattered to the floor. He bent over and his lower back seized, so he squatted, holding on to a table, fumbling for the buckle while a woman wearing a tight white blouse, blue eye shadow, and cherry red lipstick that seeped into the creases around her lips leaned toward him, leering.

"Where's Priscilla?" she said, and her husband laughed as she planted a kiss on the old man's forehead. He found the belt buckle and stood, slowly, feeling her saliva cool on his skin.

He looked at her and thought, Lord, if this was thirty years ago, I'd have you eating out of my asshole.

"Priscilla's dead," the old man said, and he walked on.

He stepped onto the stage. The crowd quieted. Ben sensed it was the sort of silence before a tragic revelation, as if someone had brought out a pan of water for Jesus and asked him to walk atop it even though everyone knew he'd get his feet wet. The old man picked up the microphone and cleared his throat.

"Where's Priscilla?" someone shouted. People laughed. The woman in the tight white blouse looked around her table because she wanted them to acknowledge that she'd said it first.

"I'll do one song and then I'm leaving," the old man said.

"'Heartbreak Hotel,'" one of the bikers shouted. The bartender called out, "'See See Rider'" and soon everyone was shouting out a song. Ben saw it amid the drunkenness and irony—an old man in a white sweatsuit clutching a gold lion's head belt buckle in one hand and a microphone in the other, with all eyes on him and people already clamoring for a better view. A throng of bikers pushed their way to the front. The blond woman with high hair took a seat atop the bar next to the bartender.

The old man cleared his throat again. "No music this time. I'm just gonna sing it myself."

He closed his eyes, tipped his head back, and sang.

Come ye weary heavy laden
Open wide stands mercy's doors
Jesus ready waits to save you
With your killers and your whores.

Come ye weary heavy laden
Lost and ruined by the fall
If you tarry till you're better
You will never come at all.

He finished and set the microphone on the PA, still clutching the lion head. Holy shit, thought Ben; the old man was crying a little.

The crowd said nothing as he hobbled off the stage. Ben rushed to help him but the old man pushed his hand away. When they got back to their corner booth, the old man fell into his seat. He wiped his eyes and laughed.

"Goddamn, that was something else," the old man said. He held up his hands, and saw they were shaking.

The bartender flicked the lights and announced last call while the old man thumbed through a fold of twenties and pinned them to the table with an empty beer mug. Their table was littered with empty peanut shells, crumpled napkins, and a menu that had a phone number written on it in red lipstick. The woman in the tight white blouse had stumbled over after the winners of the karaoke contest were announced.

"You should've won first place," she'd said to the old man. She pulled a lipstick tube from her alligator-skin purse and started writing. "Consider this your consolation prize."

Ben returned from the bathroom and slouched into the booth, yawning. Singles made their final pitches at the bar, offering whatever spoils remained—a cigarette, a recycled pickup line, a jangle of keys, an offer of a ride home.

"See that table in the middle of the room?" the old man said to Ben. "The one with two women and two men?"

Ben nodded.

"I been getting dirty looks from the big guy," the old man said. "His wife's the one gave me her phone number. Same one kissed me on the forehead when I dropped my buckle."

"Maybe there's a back door we can sneak out," Ben said, and he smiled to himself. He hadn't been this drunk in years. His seat was warm, and he wondered if he could nap for a few minutes before getting back on the road.

The old man hitched up his pants. "We're leaving through the front. But keep an eye out."

Halfway across the parking lot Ben heard a woman raise her voice, and he turned to see the big guy pull away from the woman in the tight white blouse and begin stalking across the gravel toward them. The man wore a suit but his jacket was off, tie loosened and hanging to one side. His friend walked slowly behind, looking back at his wife with his hands held out helplessly as if his feet were moving of their own accord.

The big guy jabbed a finger in the air. "You think it's okay to flirt with another man's wife?"

Ben stepped in front of the old man. "We're all a little drunk, and I think we—"

"Shut up." The big guy began rolling his sleeves. "I don't care how old he is. Doesn't give him a free pass. Step aside unless you want some—"

A tube of metal shot past Ben's face. The old man's arm was outstretched, handgun at the end.

"Walk away," the old man said.

The big guy froze, mouth open.

"I'll say it once more." The hammer clicked back. "Walk. Away."

He did as he was told, slowly, hands clenched at his sides. His wife ran up to him with arms outstretched. They hurried away in silence, disappearing beyond the fringe of the parking-lot lights.

The old man tucked the pistol into his waistband.

"What the *fuck*?" Ben said.

"It was about to get bloody. I made sure it didn't."

"Jesus Christ, you can't just pull a gun—"

"Goddamn right I can, and don't you use the Lord's name in that manner. I don't need you trying to drive with two swollen eyes from some drunk sonofabitch—"

Ben heard a *bonk* and the old man lurched forward. Tires spit gravel and a red Volvo swerved out of the parking lot. The woman with blue eye shadow was screaming at him from an open window.

"Fuck you! You don't even look like Elvis, you crazy old fuck!"

Ben caught the old man. Blood streamed down the side of his face, black under the lights.

"Someone shot me," the old man mumbled, clutching his head, eyes rolling.

Ben saw the empty beer bottle lying on the ground.

"*Nadine*," the old man whispered. He tried to stand and staggered again. Ben's legs buckled under his weight. "This is how it ends, son. I dreamt it all the time."

5.

The old man and Ben were taken to the home of Darryl Sikes, president of the local chapter of Hell's Foster Children. Darryl Sikes was a tall, thick man with hands hard as marble and blue eyes hidden deep behind red fleshy cheeks. He had a vague superhero look, Ben thought, with a square jaw and a prominent forehead and dark hair cut short for a biker. He wore a leather jacket, creased and creaky, *Hell's Foster Children* emblazoned across the back in bloodred Gothic font. A baby devil in leather diapers stood behind the *H* in *Hell*, its pitchfork making the *E*. The more Ben thought about it, the more Darryl didn't look like a biker at all. He was too refined, too coiled with muscle. He could have been a former college athlete, softened a bit by time and beer. His fellow bikers looked the part, though: long haired, dusty jeans, tan arms marked with tattoos and veins running over their biceps.

Darryl and his gang had watched the old man pull a gun on the yuppie, then watched the yuppie's wife chuck the bottle at the old man's head, and they'd all leaned back on the seats of their bikes and laughed until the old man collapsed in Ben's arms.

They'd carried the old man to his car and Ben followed Darryl to his house atop a wooded hill accompanied by a convoy of roaring bikes. In the living room of his five-bedroom new build they laid the old man on the blue-and-white striped couch and Darryl's wife, Myra, dressed the wound. The rest of the bikers stood around Darryl's living room, arms crossed, mouths tight with concern.

Ben sat in front of the fireplace, Darryl next to him in a poofy leather chair. The living room opened into a kitchen with a breakfast bar, staircase along the far wall leading to a catwalk that looked over the first floor. The house smelled of new carpet and fresh paint. The bikers had taken off their boots in the foyer. A china cabinet held little porcelain dogs, framed photos, and engraved beer mugs from Darryl and Myra's travels: Vegas, Charlotte, Raleigh, Baltimore.

"It was a damn fine performance," Darryl said to Ben. "I'm not a fan of gospel, but he made it sound good. *Real* good. Too bad he didn't win. It's a disgrace, really."

"If it's based upon stage presence, then no question he wins," one of the bikers said. "But it was Elvis night and the rules say you have to do an Elvis song."

Frank, the oldest member of Hell's Foster Children, shook his head and crossed his thick arms over his chest. His tattoos were faded, lost amid graying forearm hair. "Bullshit. The man pours his heart out onstage and you're telling me he loses to some yuppie because of Roxanne's *rules*?"

Darryl spoke to Ben while the others continued their argument.

"Where did you say you were from?"

"Cheektowaga," Ben said. "It's near Buffalo."

"I take it you two are headed to Little Valley."

"Where?"

Darryl grinned. "Little Valley, Tennessee. For the Elvis Tribute Contest. My wife and I are big fans. I know a pro when I see it. He doesn't really look like him, but he owned that stage. I mean, he *owned* it. I closed my eyes and could've sworn it was the King."

Darryl glanced over his shoulder at Myra, who sat near the old man with an ice pack pressed to his temple. The old man's eyes were closed. He looked asleep.

"So, listen." Darryl lowered his voice and leaned forward with his hands clenched together, elbows resting on his knees. "You and the old man should come with us to Little Valley. We're making a vacation out of it, Myra and me, maybe a few of the boys and their wives. We know all the good 'cue joints between here and there, and a couple places with the kind of women you'll tell stories about in your old age. It wouldn't be a lonely trip, know what I mean? What I'm trying to say is you'll get laid. We got all sorts—blond cuties with pigtails and cutoffs, long-haired brunettes with nails that'll claw the hair off your back, pierced chicks, shaved chicks, chicks with tats, fighting chicks, drinking chicks, chicks with limps and harelips—"

Ben shook his head. "I don't think we can make the detour. The old man is determined to get to Memphis."

Darryl grinned. "Of course he is. I guess you two are headed to Graceland."

"Your guess is as good as mine," Ben said.

* * *

The last time Ben saw Jessica, he knew it was over because she brought her best friend, Mindy, to their weekly lunch at Rigoletto's, an Italian bistro in the Palisade Mall with wall paintings of grape vines crawling across a sunlit field. Mindy was a doe-eyed girl with a nice laugh and a permanent ponytail, and she and Jess kept exchanging looks as if Ben didn't notice. They finished lunch and Mindy went to the restroom. Jessica started chewing her thumbnail. Ben fished ice from the bottom of his glass.

He crunched a cube. "Just say it."

"Say what?"

"Come on. I already know."

"Okay. It's over."

"Hold on. I didn't mean—"

"I'm so relieved." She smiled. "I thought for sure you'd freak."

"I am freaked."

"You don't look freaked."

"I'm freaked, Jess. Trust me."

"Well, whatever. I've said it and that's what I wanted to say, and I'm sorry for doing this in public, but I just thought you'd go crazy."

He lowered his voice. "You're seeing someone else."

"Please. I'm leaving for college in a month."

"Then wait a month."

"What's the point?"

Ben thought for a moment. "I don't know."

Jessica nodded as if to say, *Exactly*. Then she peered over her shoulder. "Here comes Mindy. Please don't put her in an awkward spot, okay?"

Mindy sat down and smiled politely. She and Jess exchanged another look—Ben realized they'd had it all planned from the start—and Mindy said, as if on cue:

"We should probably get going. It's my dad's birthday and I want to get him a tie at Harold's."

"What kind of tie?" Ben said.

"Silk."

"Italian?"

"Um, sure."

"Great," Ben said. "I'll join you. I worked at Harold's last summer."

He followed them to Harold's, to a sporting goods store where they bought a six-pack of socks, then to a soft-pretzel kiosk and a coffee shop. As they sat in the food court, drinking from paper cups and watching old people shuffle past, Mindy's cell chirped and she walked away.

Jessica grabbed Ben's arm. "What are you doing?"

"Enjoying my day."

"You're not going to change my mind."

"I know. But since this is our last date—"

"It's not a date." She let go of his arm and sat back in her chair, arms crossed, chin lowered. "Mindy thought you were really rude to our waiter at lunch."

"I hate the waiters at Rigoletto's. They always flirt with you."

"I don't even care, Ben. I really don't. You want to know why I dumped you? Because you always get like this."

"Like what? Pissed because some waiter is flirting with my girlfriend?"

"No. Like you're *desperate*. Like I'm the only thing you have going on, and now that it's over—"

"But I am desperate. I don't want this to end, so if I'm having a difficult time with it, just be patient. This is how it works, anyway."

Jessica rolled her eyes. "I don't even know what you're talking about."

"I guess I've always been desperate," Ben said, and he sipped his coffee. "Even when we first started dating. I knew this would happen, you know. Not *quite* like this . . ." Ben nodded toward the legions of mall walkers and moms with strollers. "But I've been waiting for this day. If that makes me weird—"

"It makes you pathetic."

Ben said nothing. He finished his coffee with a gulp and crumpled the cup. Then he walked away, hands in his pockets. On the way to the main concourse, he pulled Mindy aside. She covered her cell and frowned at him.

"I've always had a thing for you," he said. "Meet me tonight for dinner."

"What?"

"I know I was rude to our waiter but that's not who I am. They always flirt with Jessica—"

"*Gross,*" Mindy said. She yanked her arm from his grip and walked back to the table.

This is self-destruction at its most refined, Ben told himself. You don't even like Mindy. Jessica was right: You're pathetic, a college guy still trolling for high-school birds.

He got drunk with Patrick that night and blew off class the next day. Cheektowaga was perfect because he could go to the mall in sweatpants and no one stared. The pool of mediocrity was warm and inviting; Ben felt he could swim in it for the next ten years, just float on his back, gazing at the sky. Mall Muzak played REO Speedwagon, Aldo Nova, and Elvis's Vegas years. Fucking brilliant, thought Ben. Fucking perfect. Fucking pathetic.

* * *

They put Ben in the upstairs guest bedroom, on a high bed surrounded by lacy pillows, in a room with soft white walls and a soft white carpet. An armoire stood against the far wall, fake ivy trailing from a blue-and-white ceramic pot sitting atop the cabinet. A white teddy bear wearing a Harley Davidson leather vest lay on its side, entangled in the ivy, peeking out from its plastic jungle.

Downstairs Ben heard the laughter of Darryl and his gang. The old man was talking, joking, telling stories. Ben had left him seated on the couch, gauze taped to his temple, drinking milk from a brandy snifter ("I'll take a milk and brandy without the brandy") and eating a peanut butter and jelly sandwich ("Toast that bread dark as night and go heavy on the peanut butter").

He stared at the ceiling, smooth white glowing pale from the half-moon. It was during moments like these, Ben thought—unexpected late-night parties, laughter trilling past midnight—that his alienation surfaced at its most savage. Of course, only he remained aware of it, hiding behind a smile and understanding nods.

He didn't know where the alienation originated because it had always been with him, long before his father's death. He'd had it as a child, listening to his parents laughing and drinking in the living room with their friends, and he remembered squeezing his eyes shut as hard as he could—blossoms of white, red, and yellow dissolving and reforming in the dark—until the noise faded away, their voices retreating into soft babbles and the clink of glasses. Nothing comforted him during those late nights. Only the autistic closeness of his blanket and the rhythm of his heart in his ears.

The night he found out his father had been rammed into a hot dog stand, he left the house and drove to the driving range. He'd never golfed before, never understood the appeal of walking around a giant lawn all day, lugging a bag full of iron sticks. But that night—the phone call, the amnesiac drive to his parents' house, the confusion, the salted peanuts for dinner—he wanted to golf, the best part of golf, the only part he understood: smacking the shit out of a little white ball.

He bought ten buckets and asked the skinny kid behind the counter to give him their best driver. The kid—wearing a baseball cap and a T-shirt with *Bobby's Links* blocked across the front—snickered and said, "They're all shit," and gave Ben a chipped club with a dull face. Ben didn't care, even if he felt like taking a swing at the skinny kid's face.

He'd left his mom on the couch, with her sister and some cousins from his dad's side. He didn't think about them as he whacked ball after ball into the night, tiny white spheres zipping into the fluorescent dark like tracer fire. He didn't think about his father and the hot dog stand. He didn't think about his final year of college beginning in one week. He just swung and swung, shocked at how far the balls seemed to travel, imagining himself at long last discovering his true calling, his hidden talent unveiling a path to glory. Maybe I'm a born golfer, Ben remembered thinking that night. The first tour I win, I'll thank my dad.

The old man shook him awake.

"We're running late," he said. "We need to get to Kentucky by dusk."

Ben sat up. Morning light soaked the carpet. The old man's bandage was fresh and his hair was still wet from a shower. He wore his black bathrobe.

"There's some breakfast waiting for you," the old man said, then he left, whistling.

Ben walked downstairs. Sunlight poured through the kitchen windows. Myra stood behind the breakfast bar, her black hair wet and brushed back behind her ears. She wore a white bathrobe and pink slippers. Her face looked freshly scrubbed. Pieces of mascara clung to her eyelashes.

"Good morning," she said. "We saved you some bacon and I can put on a fresh pot if you'd like."

Ben looked around the living room. No trace of the night before. No bloodied gauze, no bikers.

"Where's Darryl?"

"At work. Coffee?"

"I'm okay." Ben sat at the bar and munched on a crinkled strip. "Where's the old man?"

"You mean Elvis."

Ben smiled but she did not.

"It's really him," she said.

He said nothing.

"It's him," she insisted. "Last night onstage—don't tell me you didn't feel something." She pulled out the dishwasher rack and began loading glasses into a cupboard. "He told me the two of you are going to rescue his granddaughter."

"That's the plan."

"Can I go with you?"

Ben paused in mid-chew. "It's not up to me. I mean, it's his granddaughter—"

"Last month my niece Rhianna died," Myra said. "When she was five the doctors diagnosed her with lymphoma and said she'd be gone in six months. That was four years ago. We'd just celebrated her ninth birthday. She couldn't hold on anymore, but she was such a little warrior." She closed the cupboard and took a deep breath. "One month after her diagnosis, we took Rhianna to Graceland and she touched that painting of the King. The one with Priscilla and Lisa Marie and he's wearing those tinted glasses—"

"Myra, he's not Elvis."

She stared at Ben. "You felt something last night. Tell me you didn't."

"I did. But that doesn't make him Elvis."

"Four years," Myra said. "The doctors gave my niece six months, and after she touched that painting she held on for four years. Now, explain that to me."

"I can't." Ben wanted to ask, *If that painting worked like you think it did, how come your niece still died?* But he kept quiet because a few months after his father's death he was convinced his father had faked it so he could leave town and start a new family. Grief made you believe the sun revolved around the earth and that kid from *Saved by the Bell* died from eating Mentos with Diet Coke and if you feed a seagull Alka-Seltzer its stomach explodes.

The old man walked into the kitchen from the back of the house. He leaned over and kissed Myra on the cheek.

"Now, is that good bacon or is that good bacon," he said. "Never liked it with the soft fat around the edges."

Ben's cell vibrated in his pocket. He looked at the number and excused himself, walking back upstairs.

"Ben?"

Downstairs he heard Myra shriek with laughter. In his mind he saw the old man feeding her a bacon strip. Inch by inch. The crumbly burnt stuff falling into her barely tied robe.

"Ben, I spoke with your father last night."

He slid down to the white carpet, his back against the side of the bed. He closed his eyes and rubbed his forehead.

"I just wanted to tell you I haven't dreamt about him in weeks, but he apologized and said he's been very busy. Very busy—can you imagine? Anyway, he wanted me to tell you that you need to be careful because apartment fires are among the top five killers of men in their mid-twenties. He said that no matter how careful you are yourself, you live in a public building and cannot control the actions of others. Chinese cooking uses a lot of oil, you know. And the Chinese are not known for their safety."

"We have smoke alarms, Mom. In every room."

"And in the stairwells?"

"Yes."

"Your father is still very concerned. Fire inspectors are over-worked and understaffed. I doubt they've come to your building within the past year."

"We had an inspection a few months ago. I requested one, after you called."

"And the inspector was thorough?"

"He seemed very competent."

"That's fine but it only takes one day to violate code. Maybe you should call for another inspection. Your father and I think it would be prudent."

"Tell Dad there's nothing to worry about. Tell him I'm being very careful."

"You can tell him yourself."

"I'd rather you tell him."

Silence. Ben counted the seconds. He could see his mom, sitting at the kitchen table, sleep lines creasing her face.

"Well, I'll make sure to let your father know. And please be careful, Ben."

"I will."

He closed his cell and rubbed his head with both hands, then pressed his thumbs into the pressure points above his ears.

The Triple Warmer Meridian, it's called. He'd read a massage book a few weeks earlier, *The Art of Erotic Massage*, copyright 1978, found in a box in the basement of his apartment building, next to piles of dirty linens, empty vegetable crates with Chinese script painted along the side (possible fire code violation), and stacks of rusted oil paint cans and turpentine (definite fire code violation). The massage book was hilarious—age-yellowed glossy paper, and the women all had enormous bush. One woman with pendulous breasts lay on a crocheted orange hammock, legs spread, her nude man standing behind her with both hands on her shoulders, both of them with the come-hither stares of professional swingers. Satisfying women isn't just about the clitoris or the G-spot, the caption insisted. It's about *kundalini*. The energy that lies dormant at the base of the spine. The dragon's fire.

He thought about calling Jess.

What's that? You want me to visit you? You know I'd love to but I can't. I'm driving Elvis to Memphis in search of his granddaughter. That's right, I said Elvis. The one and only. He even looks a little like him.

Downstairs he heard more laughter. The old man was like a light switch, Ben thought. From dark to blinding just like that.

But maybe I can stop by on my way back home. Work on your kundalini for a while. I'll bring the hammock.

Motorcycles roared into the driveway, and Ben jogged downstairs.

Darryl Sikes walked into the living room and looked around slowly. He wore his leather jacket and heavy, dark boots. His face was flushed, sweat running down his temples.

Ben stopped on the bottom step. Myra tied her robe shut. Darryl's leather jacket creaked like a redwood in a windstorm as he stomped into the kitchen and turned on the faucet.

"You're bleeding," Myra said.

He scrubbed his hands with soap. "This isn't my blood."

The gang of bikers burst through the front door. They carried a bloodied man between them. They put the man on the floor and Frank gritted his teeth.

"T-Rex hit KC in the face with a ball-peen hammer," Frank said. "Sons of bitches must pay."

Ben stared at the bloodied man. His cheek was split open and bits of tooth poked through the glistening flesh. He breathed from the other side of his mouth, swallowing blood and trying not to cough.

"They hired Screaming Eagles to bust the strike," Frank continued. "So KC dropped the first scab. Next thing we know, someone hits Petey over the head with a two-by-four."

Myra put her hand to her mouth. "Oh God, no—"

"Then T-Rex nailed KC. Didn't even give him a fighting chance. Just popped him with the hammer and let him fall."

Darryl ran his fingers through his hair and stalked around the living room. KC began to cough. Blood sprayed from his mouth and soaked into the carpet.

"Call the police," Myra said.

Darryl shook his head. "No cops."

"Darryl—"

"No cops. Not this time. We're Hell's Foster Children. This time we do it my way."

The door to the basement opened and the old man stepped into the living room. He had changed into his red sweatsuit, hair combed high, a pair of green-tinted aviator glasses resting on his sagging cheeks. He held a laundry bag in one hand and a mimosa in the other.

The old man walked around the couch. The gang of bikers stepped aside as he craned his neck to look at the man lying bleeding on the floor. He set the laundry bag down and sipped his mimosa. He stared long and hard while KC sputtered and spit, then he gulped the rest of his mimosa and wiped the dribble off his chin with his sweatshirt sleeve.

"Details," he said.

"Union hired us to protect their picket line," Darryl said. "This morning they tried to bust the strike."

The old man frowned. "You also union?"

"Some of us," Darryl said. "Local 210. Frank here is president."

"What's being built?"

"Miniature golf course," Frank said.

The old man nodded to himself. "Ben, pull the car up."

"It's already parked close," Ben said.

"Then pull it closer. My back is killing me."

The old man turned to the group and held out his empty glass. Myra took it away.

"Saddle up, boys," he said. "I'm leading a charge of the righteous."

6.

They pulled up to the construction site, led by a wisteria-on-white Caddy with a young man at the steering wheel and an old man who looked like Elvis by his side. Behind them a convoy of roaring Harleys, sun gleaming on chrome, black enamel, and mirrored sunglasses.

"You ever been in a fight?" the old man asked.

"Ninth grade," Ben said. "Bill Pippen got me into a headlock for fifteen minutes. My friends chucked basketballs at his head until he let go."

"Man, I mean a real fight. Just you and some sonofabitch trying to rip each other's heads off."

Ben thought about Patrick. "Not really."

The old man sucked air between his front teeth. "Keep your hands up and your chin low. Bend your knees. Strike fast and hard, use the strength from your *hara*."

"What's a hara?"

"The center of a man's energy. Three finger widths below the navel."

"Is that anything like a kundalini?"

"A what?"

"I'm just fucking around," Ben said. He saw the rival gang at the construction site, large men sitting on plastic chairs, their feet up on coolers.

"Get serious," the old man said. "Hara, son. Center of your power. Let's do this."

The old man pulled himself out of the Caddy and walked across the gravel parking lot. Ben walked with him, members of Hell's Foster Children close behind, Darryl and Frank in the lead.

The foreman stood by a row of Porta-Pottis, looking down at his clipboard. A circle of bikers sat on folding chairs, working their way through a twenty-four-pack. Behind them, rolls of plastic putting greens, stacked like logs. Ben saw a half-assembled wooden dragon, a Swiss clock tower, and boxes of fake bricks. He saw dozens of sand mounds like giant anthills with shovels sticking out of them.

"I understand you're using non-union labor for this job," the old man said.

The foreman looked up from his clipboard. He had the tanned, leathery face of a man who'd worked his entire adult life in construction. His arms were ropy and long, veins running from shoulder to wrist, blue on tan, with a tattoo of a screaming eagle on his forearm.

The foreman slipped his pen behind his ear. "Are you an inspector?"

"I'm a concerned citizen," the old man said.

"No shit," the foreman said.

The old man thumbed over his shoulder, toward Hell's Foster Children, who stood in a leather-clad pack. "See those men back there? Those men are the backbone of this nation. Union men who work an honest day for honest wages. Now, your ragtag bunch of mercenaries—" The old man swept his hand across the circle of men sitting in folding chairs. "I don't know where you found them, but you're better off putting them back. I'll tell you a sad story. At a show in Meridian, Mississippi, my manager hired non-union for stage construction, and wouldn't you know it, two of my backup singers fell right through the stage. One of the Jordanaires busted her ankle. Poor girl was laid out for two weeks."

"Get the fuck off my construction site," the foreman said. "Before I throw you out."

"You'd do that to an old man?"

"I wouldn't." The foreman plucked the pen from behind his ear. "But he would."

He pointed with his pen at the circle of men sitting on folding chairs. The biggest of them stood, slowly, and stretched his arms over his head. His black leather jacket had *T-REX* emblazoned across the back with a graphic of his dinosaur namesake riding a chopper.

T-Rex walked toward them and stepped in front of the foreman. "There a problem?"

"Hell's Foster Children hired a spokesman," the foreman said.

T-Rex looked the old man up and down. "Who are you supposed to be?"

"Liberace," the foreman said.

"No, he looks like that English dude with the faggot name," T-Rex said. "My mom was a fan. Dinglebat-something."

"Engelbert," the old man said. "Engelbert Humperdinck."

T-Rex grinned. "That's right. Is that who you're supposed to be?"

The old man sighed.

"Okay." The foreman put the pen back behind his ear. "T-Rex, get these two the hell out of here."

T-Rex nodded at Hell's Foster Children. "What about them?"

"Waste of time," the foreman said. "Now get to it."

T-Rex grabbed the old man's arm and the old man stepped back, lowering himself into a karate pose, feet spread wide, fists held low. Pain flared in his hips and his knees popped like cherry bombs, but he steeled himself even as sweat dripped down his sides, his leg muscles quaking in protest. Sometimes he dreamt of karate routines, the old days of sweat and taped fingers and grungy mats in California dojos with that clean white California sun you couldn't find anywhere else. Light streaming across the dojo floor, across his toes, which he saw less and less of as the years ticked by. *Well, hello there. My it's been a long, long time.*

The foreman burst into laughter and T-Rex grinned and lunged for the old man, but the old man stepped into his punch and it landed in the center of T-Rex's throat. T-Rex grabbed his neck and gagged, stumbling to his knees as the old man's green-tinted aviators fell off his face.

"Christ *almighty*, I tore a muscle," the old man said, and he clutched his side while T-Rex squirmed on the dirt, trying to catch his breath in giant whoops like the call of some prehistoric bird. Plastic lounge chairs were kicked aside and the Screaming Eagles rushed forward, knocking over their beer cans, gurgling foam into the dirt. Ben heard battle cries behind him as Hell's Foster Children joined the fray, a stampede of boots like the charge of cavalry.

"The charge of the righteous!" Ben heard the old man shout, then he raised his fists, lowered his chin, and bent his knees, and the foreman swung, and Ben's eye felt like a gong struck with a mallet.

They celebrated at Lil' Rascals Neighborhood Bar and Grill, gorging themselves on Bourbon Street shrimp, Cajun steak tips, and pitchers of Budweiser Select. The old man sat at the head of the table between Darryl and Myra. Hell's Foster Children bore the marks of battle—rips in their jackets, torn collars, busted noses. Nostrils ringed with red crust. Eyebrows matted with blood. Swollen knuckles.

Ben stood in the dark space between the restrooms marked *Bulls* and *Lambs.* He paced with his head down, cell pressed to one ear and a finger plugging his other ear.

"I just wanted to talk, Jess. That's all."

"You're not talking, Ben. You're yelling."

"Sorry. It's loud in here."

"Are you drunk?"

He shut his eyes and leaned his head against the rough wooden wall. Tiny splinters poked his cheek. His head throbbed. "I was in a biker brawl today."

Jessica gasped. "Seriously?"

Ben nodded even though he realized Jess couldn't see him.

"Did you actually hit someone?"

"I did. A few times. Knocked him down, but that was after he punched me in the face and I couldn't see out of my right eye."

Silence. He listened for dorm sounds. He could see Jess lying on her bed, feet up on the wall, playing with her long blond hair and wearing a nightshirt that reached just below the tops of her thighs. Any number of freshman dogs scratched outside her door.

Paws on her dry marker board. Whining. Tails wagging. Scrapping.

"Can you see now?" Jessica asked.

"Yeah, but my head is killing me."

"Maybe you have a concussion. My cousin got into a car accident last year and banged his head on the steering wheel and he thought he was okay, but the next morning they rushed him to the hospital because he had an aneurysm. Now his face kind of droops on one side and he can't play basketball anymore."

"I don't have an aneurysm, Jess. Don't worry."

"I'm not worried."

Ben paused. Why does this have to be so hard? he thought. Every sentence begins a journey over spikes and land mines. I always promise myself it will be the last time but it never is. "Do you have a boyfriend yet?" he asked.

Jessica sighed.

"I'm just curious."

"I know, but it's none of your business."

"So I'm supposed to pretend I don't care if you have a boyfriend."

"Do whatever you want. Just don't ask me that question, because it makes me feel weird."

"Then why are you talking to me?"

"Because we're friends and there's a million other things to talk about other than my dating life."

"No, there isn't. Your dating life is all I want to talk about. I'm sick of pretending I'm okay."

"Ben—"

"Just listen. For once just let me get this—"

"Ben, you're drunk and you're yelling at me."

"I'm not, goddammit. I'm trying to get you to listen—"

She hung up. Ben tried to calm himself, staring at a framed reproduction photo of Gene Autry hanging on the rough wooden wall. Then he dialed her again, got her voice mail, and he began to apologize for yelling but stopped himself. Too late, he thought. He already sounded stupid, justifying his emotions yet again.

He banged through the bathroom door and splashed cold water onto his face and stared at himself in the mirror. A bulge under his right eye looked like a bubble on a bad tire. The cut on his lip had finally stopped bleeding. It was scabbed over like a giant cold sore and he picked at it. Blood dotted into the sink. He grabbed a paper towel and held it to his lip.

Frank stumbled in. He swayed at the urinal and looked back at Ben.

"Where you been?"

"On the phone with my ex-girlfriend."

Frank grinned. His tooth was freshly chipped. "You should go see her. All those battle scars on your face and you'll get a sympathy fuck for sure."

"She hates me."

"So what. The hateful fucks are the best kind."

Ben looked at the paper towel. A red Rorschach of a naked embrace with Jessica. *One last time,* she would say. *But only because we used to love each other.*

Frank shook off the last drop of piss and zipped his pants. He patted Ben on the back. "Forget about her. Now get on out there before Elvis eats all the shrimp."

Frank left and Darryl walked in. He nodded at Ben and took a deep breath. He leaned back against the bathroom wall, squinting at the flickering fluorescent light panels. He'd taken off his jacket, muscles shifting and tensing beneath his black T-shirt.

"What are you doing?" Darryl said.

Ben pressed the paper towel to his lip. "Nothing."

"That's cool," Darryl said quietly, to himself. He swallowed hard.

They stood in silence, echoes of their breathing in the bathroom. Darryl continued to stare at the fluorescent light panels. Ben saw dirt streaks on his jeans, something dark on his right knuckles that may have been blood but could also be barbecue sauce. Finally Ben asked, "Are you okay?"

Darryl nodded. "I'm okay."

"Are you hurt?"

"Hurt?"

"The fight," Ben said. "Did you get—"

Darryl snorted. "I'm fine. Not a scratch. Jesus, do I look like the kind of guy who'd have a hard time in a fight?"

"Not at all."

Darryl glanced at Ben. "You got it pretty good."

"I'm not much of a fighter."

"So he's the real deal, isn't he?"

"Who?"

"The old man. Don't fucking lie to me and say he isn't. He's got my wife dripping wet. She'd blow him in the coat closet if he asked."

Ben took the paper towel off his lip. He looked in the mirror, Darryl still leaning against the bathroom wall, hands in his pockets, broad shoulders bulging with useful muscle. Ben imagined what he'd do to the old man. *Slaughter* wasn't accurate enough.

"Yeah, it pisses me off," Darryl said, answering a question

Ben thought but didn't dare ask. "The other guys . . . they like his stories, his attitude. How he clocked that prick in the throat. But they don't believe. Not like I do."

Darryl walked to the urinal, slowly, unzipping his pants. He leaned one hand against the tile. Ben heard the trickle of urine.

"I have to ask myself if I can let her go," Darryl continued. "If it's worth it for him. You know, I almost caught one of his shows in Raleigh. I was sixteen. We were going as a joke, like a trip to the zoo to see some animal you never seen before. Our car broke down and we ended up selling our seats to the tow guy. Couple years later the King died. Well, that's what we all thought, anyway."

Darryl zipped his pants. He washed his hands next to Ben, looking at his reflection.

"I love Myra but I can't stop her," Darryl said. "I just hope he takes me along."

"What's the craziest thing you ever done on tour?"

The old man wrinkled his forehead and leaned back. The neon *open* sign was dark and the kitchen door was propped open, shouts and laughter from the kitchen staff floating out. The bartender had taken off his vest and he drank with a couple of young waitresses.

"I killed a man in Nevada," the old man said.

Frank lowered his voice. "Like murder?"

"Like self-defense." The old man picked through his plate of shrimp tails. "My show was over and we were driving back to the hotel, and we stopped at a traffic light. Some sonofabitch pulled Fike out of the car. Just ran up to the car and pulled him right out.

Threw him to the ground and started kicking the shit out of him. So I jumped into the front and popped that car into reverse, then gunned it and hit that sonofabitch so hard, he spun around like a top. Ran over Fike's leg, too. But Fike was okay. Four weeks in a cast and he was right as rain."

Ben sat at the other end of the table. He could barely see the old man through the crowd that had gathered around, filled with waiters, bikers, and even a few patrons. They sat, stared, laughed, and clapped, and the old man cruised through his stories and told corny jokes and some actually liked the stories and corny jokes but most didn't know why they were still there. Only that they couldn't leave because they'd never met anyone like this old fox with black hair combed high, a gash on his forehead, and claw marks on his neck from the construction site rumble.

"Took that poor man two months to die," the old man said. "I say *poor* because even though some people pissed me off to the point where I wanted them strung up by their balls—pardon my language, ladies—I never wished death on anyone. So I sent his family a fleet of white Lincolns. And signed copies of Rajmendahi's *The Transcendent Soul*. You ever read Rajmendahi? Man, he was something else. Met him backstage in Jersey City, 1973. Little guy, about five foot tall, voice like a girl. You never heard nobody wise as that man. Told me first they ignore you, then they make fun of you, then they fight you, and then you win. You get that?"

The crowd nodded.

"Then you win," the old man repeated. Myra inched closer, resting her hand on the old man's knee under the table. Ben saw Darryl sitting on the other side of his wife, staring passively.

"Do you believe in destiny?" Myra asked.

The old man shrugged. "Only Destiny I know was a black

hooker in Tupelo. We're born, we die, and there ain't no plans made by anyone other than us. There's your destiny."

The old man began to sing to himself, softly: *"All things are ready, come; come to the supper spread; come, rich and poor; come, old and young; come, and be richly fed . . ."*

"Tell us about Lisa Marie," one of the waiters said, winking at his friend.

The old man stopped. His face darkened. "I was in the middle of a song."

"I know," the waiter said. "But have you spoken to her—"

"My daughter is my business," the old man said. "Now, let me get back to my song."

The waiter ran to the back office and when he returned he was grinning. Suddenly "Viva Las Vegas" blared through the mini-speakers perched in the high corners of the room.

Everyone laughed and applauded, but the old man kicked himself away from the table and hefted an empty pitcher. "Turn that goddamn shit off!" he bellowed. When no one moved, he threw the pitcher toward the bar and it crashed into a row of liquor, shattering the Budweiser mirror. The bartender ducked and cracked his head on the side of the bar, and Ben watched him slump to the floor, blood streaming down his forehead.

The waiter backed away, stammering, "I thought—"

"Turn off that fucking music or I'll break your goddamn neck," the old man yelled, and he kicked his chair. The muscle in his side seized again; he wished he could reach into his flesh and rip it out. Rip out everything that was failing him. Don't need them anymore, he thought. Just get me to Nadine on two legs and I'll take care of the rest. I'm a juggernaut. Old and creaky but still a goddamn juggernaut.

Ben was at his side as one of the waitresses cradled the bartender's head. The manager screamed at everyone to leave. The old man kicked a table and it squawked across the floor. Darryl shoved the manager, "Viva Las Vegas" still blaring, and Ben tried to usher the old man to the door but he yelled and spat. Every time Ben grabbed his arm, the old man ripped it free. "Goddammit, I was singing and you go and put that shit on," the old man shouted, and they exited into the night, where the parking lot blacktop was still warm, smelling of tar, their shoes making whispery scuffles.

Ben rested his head on the steering wheel. He heard the old man breathing hard next to him. The old man coughed.

"I can't do this," Ben said.

"Sure you can. Just start the car and drive away."

"I think I should leave when we get to Fort Thomas," Ben said. "You don't have to pay for my ticket back. I want you to take the money and pay for those bottles you smashed—"

"They already have my money. I gave them a grand to keep the bar open."

"What about the bartender?"

"What about him."

"He's fucked up and he didn't do anything wrong. He was just standing there."

The old man coughed again. "The world is full of fucked-up people who were just standing there. Colonel was slicker than a greased snake, but I'll never forget the night after my momma died. I told him she sacrificed everything and what did she get in return, and Colonel said it isn't about who deserves what, it's about *timing*."

In his side-view Ben saw the bikers pour out of Lil' Rascals.

They stood in front of their bikes, yelling at the manager and his gang of waiters.

"Timing's what got me into those terrible movies," the old man said. "Every one of them names they gave me sounded like a gay porn star. Clint Reno. Lucky Jackson. Rick Richards. Don't tell me the writers didn't know what they were doing. My movies were a fucking joke. Turned me into a good ol' boy with a stupid grin. That wasn't what I was about. *That wasn't why I came into this world.*"

Someone banged on the passenger window. Myra. Her black hair rested on her shoulders and her teeth shone white.

The old man rolled down the window. Myra adjusted the bag slung over her arm. She raked her hair back, turning her head to let its thickness shine in the parking lot light.

"We're rambling," the old man said. "Be a darling and thank Darryl for all his hospitality."

"Take me with you," she said.

The old man smiled kindly and pulled the gold lightning-bolt ring off his finger. "I need you to do something for me."

"Anything."

He placed the ring in Myra's hand and closed her fingers over it. "I need you to give this to the bartender. Will you do that?"

Myra nodded, her eyes rimmed with tears. "Can I go with you? Please?"

The old man touched Myra's face. She closed her eyes.

"Darling, one hundred years ago you'd break my heart," he said, then he gestured to Ben, who started the car and pulled away. In his rearview he watched Myra fade from red to black, standing in the parking lot with her weekend bag as the old man began to sing again.

* * *

It stormed all night into the next day, cedar trees swaying against the dark flashing sky. They'd driven past Fort Thomas, along narrow Kentucky roads bounded by stone walls and plank fences. The Caddy's wipers weren't fast enough and the water fell in sheets but Ben still drove. His right eye was blacked and swollen; the knuckles of his right hand were cut in the shape of someone's teeth.

The old man kept quiet. His green-tinted aviators sat crooked on his face, one arm missing, the crinkled map spread across his lap with doughnut crumbs collected in the center crease.

"Everyone has a lost love." The old man stared out the window at the raindrops shuddering across the glass. "I lost mine in Tupelo. Emma Grant. Wasn't the prettiest I'd been with, but man, she was the sweetest. Told me she'd take care of me until the end of my days. I still remember what she looked like when no one was watching."

He turned to Ben. "That's when you see right into someone's soul. How they look in their private moments. First thing in the morning she'd think I was asleep, and she'd sit by the bedroom window. Way the sunlight touched her face, you'd think it had to ask permission. Long golden hair and the whitest skin I ever seen. Like fresh cream. One green eye and one blue. And her hands . . ."

He held up one bruised hand.

"Fingers like a china doll. Soft skin put me to sleep every time it touched my face. Couldn't even make love to her because it would've been obscene, until one night she begged and begged and so I obliged. And now it's her granddaughter I'm going to save."

The old man took off his aviators.

"Emma had a daughter named Gladys. Named after my mother. I was at Gladys's christening, in a small church on the banks of

Otter Creek. Eighteen years ago Gladys had herself a daughter. Nadine Emma Brown. I used to send money but I stopped, and if you held a gun to my head, I couldn't tell you why. But I blame myself for Nadine's fall from grace."

Ben swerved around a fallen branch thick as an elephant's leg. The old man put his aviators back on.

"Priscilla told me I'd be the ruin of everyone I love. Told me everything I'd gained would be their loss. God only gives so much before He takes, you understand. God isn't about good versus evil. He's about balance. Give a penny, take a penny. The blind can hear a fly taking a shit; the deaf can stand in the clubhouse and see a blade of grass on the eighteenth hole. And if you believe that, let me tell you about a hooker in Duluth who sucks dick so goddamn good, she gives one out of three men heart attacks."

The old man laughed to himself, fist held to his mouth with his head down as if he were listening to the laughter of his previous life. Then sadness washed over his face, and once again he leaned his head against the window.

"But I'm being serious now," he said. "Without balance the whole thing falls apart because the sun always melts the wings of motherfuckers flying too high. September 1976 I dreamt of a grinning beast walking through the desert with a six-shooter and a bottle of whiskey. I'm sitting in the shadow of a giant red rock eating at a big table, a big old feast all for me. Then I hear its spurs jangling and the cylinder on its six-shooter is clicking round and round, and it kicks over a cactus and takes a swig of whiskey, pointing the six-shooter between my eyes. It throws its head back and howls and says, *Boom*." The old man shuddered. Rain spat against the windshield. "That's why I left. When I left God turned away. But now that I'm alive again, God's taken notice.

The beast howling thirty years ago slouches toward Memphis, waiting to be born."

The old man tore open a bag of pretzels and stuffed a handful into his mouth. He chewed slowly, crumbs tumbling down the front of his ripped red sweatshirt.

"My teeth hurt," he said through a mouthful. "One of those bikers clocked me good." He looked at Ben over the top of his aviators. "You got the worst of it, though."

"Thanks. I'm not much of a fighter."

"It's the spirit that counts, son."

The road curved and dipped. A truck screamed past, throwing spray.

"What's her name?" the old man asked.

Ben glanced over at him.

"I saw you tighten when I said everyone has a lost love. What's her name?"

"Jessica."

"This the one that dumped you?"

Ben nodded.

"Never met an ugly girl named Jessica," the old man said.

"She was beautiful," said Ben. "I'm still not sure what she saw in me. She could've been with someone taller."

The old man sang quietly. "*Our love is oft-times low, our joy still ebbs and flows—*"

"It's not that I can't get women like Jessica," Ben continued. "I just can't keep them. Once they figure out my game, it's over."

"*But peace with Him remains the same, no change Jehovah knows.*"

"How old was she?" the old man asked, and he went back to singing. "*I'll never forget the night you told me—*"

"Seventeen."

The old man whistled. "Man, those young ones are like kittens. Always looking for something new to play with. Trick is you have to be the one to walk away first. Kittens don't chase string that lies on the floor. They chase the string that pulls away."

"So I shouldn't call her anymore?"

"Hell, no. Sobbing won't make a seventeen-year-old girl take you back."

"Well, I wasn't going to *sob*—"

"Young girls live in mythology." The old man brushed crumbs off his shirt. "Their music, their movies, their relationships. Heartbreak makes them feel grown-up. Nothing a young girl wants more than to feel grown-up, and she'll lay waste to anyone for the taste of a broken heart."

7.

*T*hree women sat in a corner booth in the Coyote Café roadside bar with a sign above the kitchen door that read *If You Send Anything Back We'll Spit in It Again.* The room was small and noisy, rough pine walls covered in custom license plates with various rock star names (Hendrix, Jagger, Lennon), and framed photos of Marilyn Monroe, Babe Ruth, and Joe Namath. Beer posters showed busty cartoon beer maids dripping froth from giant mugs. A chandelier hung in the middle of the dance floor, a ten-armed gold ball with colored bulbs at the end of each arm. The jukebox was lit with strobing LED.

The three women wore khaki shorts and pastel tanks, tanned legs shiny with lotion. They were all barefoot, toenails painted in shades of pink, sandals in a pile under the table. Fiona—freckles, long black hair, and a toothy grin—stared at her friend.

"So what would you do if a cute guy walked into this restaurant," Fiona said, "and gave you that look?"

Alex pushed her blond hair behind her ears. A thin scar ran across her upper lip. "What look?"

"*That* look," Fiona said. "You know the look I'm talking about."

"I wouldn't do anything."

"You wouldn't give him a look back."

"Absolutely not."

Fiona slid her feet off Alex's booth cushion and let them slap onto the plank floor.

"Oh, that's such bullshit." Fiona frowned at Heather sitting next to her. "Alex used to be an honest girl. I don't know what happened."

Heather sipped her Coke. Fiona put her feet back up.

"Would you call Derek if he called you?" Fiona asked.

Alex paused. "Yes."

"And what would you say to him."

"Depends on what he'd say to me."

"What if he apologized?"

"Then I'd take him back."

"She's still in love," Heather said, and she wrinkled her nose at the Coke fizz. "Leave her alone."

"I say she's not in love," Fiona said. "I say she doesn't know what love is."

Alex raised an eyebrow. "And you do?"

"I never said that. But I know what love isn't. Love isn't a boyfriend who fucks someone else while his girlfriend is at the hospital taking care of her mother."

"*Ouch*," Heather said.

Alex looked away. "It was a difficult time for everyone."

"Nuh-uh." Fiona waved her index finger. "Derek doesn't get that free pass. You have to earn that free pass, and Derek didn't."

"He came by, every day."

"Until he met *her*. And then he gave you excuses."

Alex set her drink down and stared hard at Fiona. "It was a difficult time for everyone."

Fiona leaned back, arm draped over the back of their booth. "Not for Derek it wasn't, and that's all I'm going to say."

They walked in, the old man in front and Ben behind. Ben immediately saw the girls laughing in their booth and wondered if he'd ever become the kind of man who approaches three laughing women. They took a table by the dessert cooler. Ben pushed the menu away because he was sick of eating. Every few hours they'd stopped somewhere for food. The old man always left hundred-dollar tips. Ben kept his cell on vibrate, checking it every hour.

He realized that calling Jessica had been a mistake. His obsessiveness was like a rash he'd finally covered with a bandage, but after two days with the old man, he'd ripped it off and tore into the still-red skin. Six months didn't matter anymore; it was as if she'd just left him.

He wanted her back and he wanted vengeance and he wanted everything he didn't have. A new girlfriend; a new car; a mom who didn't speak to her dead husband every night. The five thousand sitting in the trunk of the old man's Caddy was the biggest lump sum he'd ever received, and it was almost big enough for the scope of his ambition. The other five thousand he'd receive if he drove the old man all the way to Memphis would be enough to launch his dream.

That apartment in Amsterdam, Ben reminded himself. Something small and chic, with cool lighting and grown-up furniture. A place where he could smoke hash on the balcony, greeting the day with the insouciance of the very young and the very rich. He'd take up some sort of painting class and do what he imagined every other twenty-something expat did: Invite some half-bored, half-intrigued Dutch thirty-something back to his apartment for nude portraits, fucking her doggy-style on the balcony by the fourth session while watching the sun set over the canals.

If I could do that, Ben thought, Jessica would be a dim memory.

But he knew what would happen. Even if he got that apartment and that cool lighting and that grown-up furniture, and even if he managed to take himself seriously enough to try the bullshit young-artist gig, and even if by some wild reality-storm he charmed a Dutch thirty-something enough to make her grab hold of a balcony railing while he pounded away, he would still find a way to fuck it up.

The old man caught Ben staring at the three girls on the other side of the room.

"Last pit stop I called an old friend down in Memphis," the old man said. "Eddie Fulsom. Played bass with Junior Kimbrough. Eddie owns a car-parts store now but he used to consort with the local criminal element—put his fingers in the pot but never got his hands dirty, if you know what I mean."

Ben nodded but he wasn't listening. He was watching Alex, the girl with long blond hair and a thin scar running through her upper lip. She stood and walked across the room, barefoot. The chandelier colored her face red as she passed under it.

"We'd like some refills," Ben heard Alex say to the young waitress who was behind the counter talking to another young waitress.

The waitress hooded her eyes. "I'll bring some over in a minute."

"How about now? We've been waiting for a while."

"In a minute." The waitress snapped her gum.

Alex walked back to the table and grabbed their three glasses. She pushed past the waitress to the soda machine.

"You're not allowed back here."

"Then call the manager." Alex refilled each glass and held them up for her friends. Fiona and Heather clapped while soda spilled over the side. Alex stuck out her tongue and licked it off her wrist.

"Eddie's heard some things about Nadine," the old man continued. "Gave me a name: Hank Rickey. Hank goddamn Rickey. You ain't never seen a more unholy man in all your life, like he was put on this earth to fight and fuck. Then Hank saw God in an oil slick on his driveway in 1952 and swore it all off. At least that's how the story goes."

The old man tugged on the cuff of his red sweatshirt.

"Not many people know my version of 'That's All Right' was Hank's. Crudup wrote it, but what made it special wasn't Phillips, like everyone thinks. Wasn't Scotty or Bill, and it sure as hell wasn't me. Hank could've sang that song and it would've taken off like nothing you've ever seen. Same with 'Blue Moon of Kentucky' and 'Baby Let's Play House.' Forget everything you know about me—Hank done it a hundred times better. But like I said: He saw God in an oil slick and gave it all away."

Ben looked at the old man. "I'll be right back," he said, and the old man kept quiet because he'd seen the boy staring at that leggy blonde licking soda off her wrist.

Ben slowed as he walked by their table. Fiona crunched an ice cube.

"So where are you and Elvis headed?" she said.

Ben smiled. "Memphis."

"Are you his manager?"

"I'm his driver."

"Like his chauffeur?"

"Like his driver."

"What's the difference?"

"The uniform," Ben said. "And Elvis sits in the front seat."

"Did you get into an accident or something?" Heather asked.

"A biker punched me in the face. But I think it makes me look tough."

"I think it makes you look like you got punched in the face," Alex said.

"Same difference. I'm Ben, by the way."

The three girls introduced themselves. Ben leaned against the seat-back and tried to look casual. Take a seat, he told himself. Act like you belong. Order some beers. Do *something*, for fuck's sake.

"So, Ben," Fiona said, "how long are you going to stand there?"

"Until it feels awkward."

Fiona nodded. "Well, it's getting to that point."

Ben smiled, unsure of what to say, then he mumbled, "Excuse me," and continued to the restroom.

Fiona raised her eyebrows at Alex. "Remember when I asked what you would do if a cute guy walked into this restaurant, right now, and gave you that look?"

Alex nodded.

"That's *exactly* the look I was talking about," Fiona said. "Even if he is a little weird."

Ben stood in the last stall and checked his cell. Black marker on the inside of the door: *Jenna fucked Trey and didn't even get me a shirt.* He called his home voice mail, praying Patrick wouldn't pick up. There was a message from Steve's girlfriend, Samantha, asking if he'd gone back to Broome for the summer. He ran his hands through his hair and took a deep breath and convinced himself not to call Jessica, that the old man was right and she was a kitten and he needed to be the string that pulls away, then he called her and hung up after three rings.

He thought about Alex. She had blue eyes and full lips. She was the kind of girl who didn't mind walking across a bar in bare feet. She was cute. No, he told himself. More than cute; she was *confident*. They all were, even the quiet one who just sat there and sipped her Coke. Three cute, confident women, the type who waited for men to approach them, and were perfectly content if no man did.

Get it together, Ben told himself. Women can smell desperation. Don't be Desperate Guy. Don't even be Playing-It-Cool Guy. Just walk out there and smile a little and keep walking until you get back to your table and wait for them to get a little drunk. Which should happen by . . .

He looked at his cell. Five P.M. Happy hour.

He fixed his hair, frowning in the mirror at his cut lip and black eye. Then he took another deep breath, shoved his hands into his pockets, and banged the restroom door open with his shoulder, sauntering out, the most casual guy in the state of Kentucky.

The old man sat at the table with the three women. They all had beers.

"There he is." The old man raised his mug to Ben. "Dropped three bikers with one punch. Sonofabitch saved my life."

At some point Ben had walked with Alex to the bar to help her bring back another round, and at some point they'd stayed at the bar with their margaritas getting warm and the rum and Coke losing its fizz. Alex was a little drunk, her expressions lingering, soft smiles and lazy laughter that confirmed for Ben everything he loved about women.

"Amsterdam is amazing," Alex said. "I went with my cousin a few years ago. Did you know their Kit Kats taste better than ours?"

"I didn't."

"Well, they taste a lot better. Everything tastes better in Europe." She tipped back her margarita. "So when do you think you'll go?"

Ben shrugged. "Depends on the money. I'm suburban poor. Just enough money to buy good shoes, but not enough to travel, or make any significant life change. I live in a middle-class ghetto. The mall is my hood."

"Plan it anyway," she said. "That way you'll have no choice. I'm serious. Take a bartending job for a few months and book your ticket. I'll give you my cousin's e-mail—he knows some real-estate agents there."

"Okay."

Alex gave him a wary side-glance. "You won't do it."

"Sure I will."

"No, you won't. Everyone talks but no one does."

"I don't need the bartending job. The old man's paying me ten grand to drop him off in Memphis."

"Ten *grand*? Just for driving him to Memphis?"

"It's crazy. He's already paid me half."

Alex shook her head. "That is crazy. So do you really think he's Elvis?"

Ben folded his arms atop the bar and leaned over his

margarita. "I don't know. He sang at this karaoke contest and people were shoving each other to get close to the stage. And it wasn't like they were watching a freak show. It was like they wanted to believe it was really him."

"But do you?"

"I think he's a little nuts. Not that Elvis wasn't."

"There is something about him," Alex said. "But if that's really Elvis"—she nodded at the booth where the old man sat with Heather. They were both laughing as Fiona danced to Al Green's "Look What You Done for Me"—"then we should call the *Enquirer* or something. They'd pay us ten million dollars for that scoop."

"I could buy an estate in Amsterdam," Ben said. "You could visit with your friends. Only your girlfriends, of course."

Alex grinned and took another long sip from her glass. "I don't think my boyfriend would like that."

"Tell him I'm harmless." Ben laughed and caught himself. Easy, there, he thought. Kittens and string.

Alex put down her drink and stretched her arms overhead. Her tank lifted a little; Ben caught a glimpse of her flat, tanned stomach.

"Come dance with me." She grabbed Ben's hand and pulled him from the bar.

"I can't dance like Fiona," he said.

"Good. You'd look like a girl suffering for male attention."

They danced, and at some point Heather was near them, twirling with her arms held out while she shut her eyes. The old man sat in the booth and drank as Fiona dropped to the floor and tried to stand on her head, before tottering over and crashing into a chair.

She sat up in a tumble of thick dark hair and the biggest mouth Ben had ever seen, screaming with laughter as tears ran down her freckled cheeks. Heather kept her eyes shut, twirling like a dervish surfer girl. Alex snaked her arms around Ben from behind, and he realized he didn't know if he'd left his cell phone on, but he didn't care.

8.

The old man waited outside the roadside bar with one leg propped on the porch railing. It was still raining, fat drops *plink-plinking* in parking lot puddles and tapping on the hood of his Caddy. Clouds the color of wet cement sat in a line atop a ridge of forested mountains, darkening as the sun set. The old man tried rolling a bottle cap across his knuckles, but his fingers had grown stiff with arthritis and the joints felt like they were stuffed with glue. He stared at the back of his hands, wrinkled skin as old as anything he'd ever seen.

He was content to think of nothing. Just sit back like a dog waiting for its master to return home. He heard Ben laughing with the three beautiful ladies. Good for him, the old man thought. Boy is carrying around some goddamn weight that he can't figure. Too serious for someone his age. Reminded the old man of himself, an impatient tragedian who looked for meaning the moment he understood he'd get old and die. The moment his mother got pale and quiet and the adults bowed their heads, silent in the way animals get before a storm.

Two days after his mother's death, Hank Rickey had come to the house while he lamented in his room. Besides his father, Hank was the only one he allowed to sit across from him and hold his hand while he sobbed so hard he thought he'd puke up his stomach—orange juice, pills, squirmy wet sack, and all.

· He was twenty-three going on twelve and his mother was dead. He knew his mother never liked his music, the crowds, or the girls he flirted with but never so much as stuck a finger in, and his father never amounted to any sort of an opinion, content to go whichever way, like sea grass in the tide. But as hard as it was, he told Hank, he had to keep on because of the *obligation*. The obligation to what he saw as his destiny. Who else could serve God's will? Who else had that hunger that could only come from a childhood of poverty and mother-fed narcissism? And for fuck's sake, who else had that hair and those puppy dog eyes?

I do, Hank said. I could take your place.

The old man remembered looking at Hank through the blur of tears, his handsome face distorted into a demon's mask: one eye higher than the other, full lips yanked into a cruel sneer. How in the hell could you do that? the old man remembered asking. You've given your life over to God and I've already got a couple gold singles under my belt.

Six months with my voice and the fans won't remember you, Hank had said. Only if you want, of course. Otherwise, I'm content doing what I'm doing.

The old man remembered his terror that night when the house quieted and the candles were snuffed. He lay alone in a grotesque mound of teddy bears, those gruesome fucking things with their mannequin eyes and outstretched limbs. Since that stupid song they'd never stopped coming via crate and mail, thrown over the gates of his home at all hours.

I could take your place, Hank had said. And the terror was that he could. Better face, better voice, better hair, better everything. It had all been Hank's. The hip swivel. The sneer. The gum-chewing, microphone-belching, pink-Cadillac-driving, rambling rockabilly swagger. Hank invented it all for an audience of one, for the kid with the shock of thick black hair and a high wavery voice, and Hank had told the kid he could take whatever he liked because it meant nothing anymore, not since God zapped Himself into that oil slick and demanded he live a chaste life.

That night, lying among the teddy bears, the old man resolved that if Hank ever renounced his vow and laid claim to his rightful place atop the world—and he remembered that despite everything he still considered his success the greatest con perpetrated since Judas shared matzoh with Jesus—he'd shoot Hank dead. Else the whole motherfucking party would be shut down in the time it takes the DJ to put the needle on the record.

An AMC Gremlin pulled up to the Coyote Café, tires crackling over wet gravel. The old man snapped out of his reverie and reached for his wallet. A young man stepped out of the car. He wore a jean jacket, hair straight and long down the back of his neck.

"You John Barrow?"

The old man held up a thick fold of bills. "You Luke?"

"That's right." Luke stepped onto the porch. He took the money and counted it slowly, licking his fingers.

"The bartender promised me good product," the old man said.

"No worries. I've known Jimmy for years."

"Years, huh. How old are you?"

"Twenty-six."

When Luke finished counting he fished a small orange plastic bottle from the pocket of his jean jacket and handed it over. The old man shook a handful of pills into his wrinkled palm.

"These blue ones Darvocet?"

"That's right."

"It doesn't say Darvocet."

"They're generic."

"I suppose that Placidyl's generic, too."

"Placi-what?"

The old man shook his head. "Goddammit, if I wanted generic, I'd have ordered this shit from Canada." He starting pacing, and his shirt lifted a little, flashing the pistol tucked into his waistband. "Just what the hell am I supposed to do with a bunch of no-name pills?"

Luke held up his hands, backing down the porch steps.

"The problem, Luke—you listening?—is we don't know if the lab techs put the right meds into the right containers. And don't tell me there's no difference between Dilaudid and Lortab and Phenobarbital, because there's contraindications to consider. There's the issue of dosage and timing, tolerance and allergy. People pay good money for name brands because they like to know what they're getting, and I'll be damned if I'm going to depend on some fucking Canuck that doesn't know the difference between a barbiturate and an opioid. You get me?"

"Hey, no problem." Luke dropped the fold of bills onto a step. "My mistake, so it's free of charge."

The old man frowned. "I don't want a refund. I want what I paid for."

"I'll send someone. You keep those and I'll send someone with name brands."

"Promise?"

Luke nodded and hurried into his car. As he peeled away the old man bent to retrieve the money, slowly, hands on his lower back. He knew the hippie was lying. He'd send no one. Those days were long gone. Those days when he could pick up the phone at three in the morning and have a private nurse at his bedroom door in less than an hour, wearing sheer thigh-highs and carrying a purse full of goodies.

These will have to do, the old man said to himself, and he pinched a wad of pills from his palm, dry-swallowing them with a practiced wince. Then he leaned against the porch railing and whistled an old Rufus Thomas tune.

They sat in the corner booth. Heather slumped against the wall, eyes closed. Fiona flirted with a tall man in a cowboy hat at the end of the bar. Ben stared into his glass, at twin slivers of floating ice. Alex rested her head on his shoulder and spun her empty glass round and round.

"I think about her all the time," Ben said. "I don't want to but I can't help it. It's like every day that passes is a little death— another day we're not together, another day she's talking with somebody else. I can see years from now when we're both old photos in each other's minds—"

"I hate photos," Alex said. "Every time someone shows me pictures of places they've been and people they know, it's like listening to an inside joke. I don't get it."

"Maybe Jess will regret leaving me and maybe she won't," Ben said. "But I'll always wonder. That's what kills me."

"You might not always wonder."

"I will."

"You might not. I don't regret leaving Derek."

Ben laughed to himself. "If I see a pretty girl standing in line at the grocery store, I wonder what it would be like if we got married. When she leaves the store I wonder if I'll ever see her again. It's like I get nostalgic for experiences I never had. I've already planned our little tragedy: Boy meets hot girl in some roadside bar, they drink, they talk, boy leaves because he's made a promise to an old man. But boy always wonders about that hot girl, and one day, years later, he returns to the roadside bar, looking for her. But she's long gone."

Alex yawned, readjusting her head on his shoulder. "Maybe you like being sad."

"No. I hate being sad. I hate being wounded."

"But society wants you to be sad," said Alex. "After my mom died I realized it's one of the few times in life when total self-absorption is considered okay. If you're happily self-absorbed, you're an asshole, but if you're sad . . . Hey, people may not want to be around you, but at least you don't threaten their delusions by being all happy. There's a whole culture built around sadness. It makes you feel like a part of something bigger. That's why they have grief counseling groups, and support groups where people share their sorrows. There aren't any happy groups, where people meet every week and tell each other all the great things that happened since the last meeting. And don't tell me it's because most of our life is suffering. They don't have happy groups because nobody wants to hear how happy your week was."

Ben swirled his rum and Coke, listening to the ice clink. "How did your mom die?"

"Cancer. How about your dad?"

Ben took a sip and spit it back into the glass. "Car accident."

"This is where you say let's get out of here," Alex said.

"I can't."

"Because it's not in your little tragedy."

"Because the old man is crazy about getting to Memphis. I haven't had a full night's sleep since we left. He'll want to keep driving through the night."

"I see."

"We should meet up in Memphis, though. Or Amsterdam."

"Maybe," Alex said.

"Shit," Ben said. "Did I blow it?"

Alex sat up and kissed him, long enough to show him what he was missing. When she finished she pulled away, his mouth still open, and she said, "You did, but I'll let it slide."

Then she stood, slowly, holding on to the seat-back for balance, and slinked her way across the bar, disappearing into the bathroom.

Ben closed his eyes. One week ago if a woman with long blond hair, sparkling blue eyes, and a fearless kind of tomboy sexiness had pulled him onto a roadhouse dance floor with her hot, drunk friends, he would have driven his Honda hatchback through a nursery school to follow that woman wherever she was headed.

But not now, he thought. His world was shrinking. Just him, the old man, and their Caddy. A mission from God, the old man had said, and Ben didn't believe him but it began to sound good. Good because it was something different.

I'm doing something greater than looking for random hookups, Ben thought. I'm on an actual mission. The first mission of my life. It's something people want to be a part of. But it's just us.

The old man stumbled in through the front door. His clothes were soaked with rain and hair stuck to his forehead. Black hair dye ran into his eyes; he kept wiping them even as he scanned the room.

"Been wasting our time." The old man pitched forward and caught himself on the back of a booth. "God sent me for Nadine and look what we're doing."

Alex emerged from the bathroom and walked past the old man, staring warily at him as he shook a finger at Ben.

"Hank's come back to reclaim what was his," the old man said. "Can't have me, so he's gone for my granddaughter. No telling what that motherfucker will do. No time to spare. We have to get her."

Ben looked at Alex. "Give me your number. Before he completely loses it."

Alex smiled. "You were so much better when you played coy."

"I wasn't playing. I am coy."

"Why's that?"

"Because I'm wounded."

Alex smiled again. "Okay. But don't use your wounded excuse for that waiting-three-days-to-call bullshit."

hottest grl evr wanted 2 fuck and I said no

b/c u r gay

no b/c elvis freaked

what?

"Eyes on the road," the old man said.

call u later, Ben typed to Patrick then closed his cell. He'd asked the old man for a break—a few hours at a motel, a few hours at a rest stop, or even another sit-down at a diner so he could nap in the booth. But the old man said they needed to get to a town called Eden before nightfall. Ben asked him what was in Eden. The old man wouldn't answer. Instead he clutched the coffee-ring-stained manila envelope lying across his lap, set his mouth in a hard line, and closed his eyes, and Ben thought he was asleep until he tried to pull over. Then the old man's eyes snapped open and he told Ben to keep going. All day if he had to, until they got to Eden.

They drove under sagging boughs of beech and white basswood, over pitted roads, past misty green forests dripping warm rain. The AC didn't work and Ben's shirt was soaked through. The old man's face dripped sweat. His speech slurred and his eyes rolled in their sockets, and he grew restless, switching on the radio to a gospel station.

They drove past swollen streams where branches bent against the rushing water, the forests dark despite the sun bullying its way through storm clouds. The old man turned up the radio until the speakers buzzed, and he sang as loud as he had in forty years, bellowing his faith in the Lord and warning the devil to seek shelter elsewhere because his heart was filled with the love of God.

And then he stopped suddenly and looked at the address scrawled on the back of a restaurant napkin. He checked the map, then grabbed the wheel and jerked it, the Caddy swerving off the road, spitting muddied gravel that popped against the windshield. Ben cursed and pulled the wheel back, but he was already at the end of a narrow driveway that disappeared up ahead in a tangle of trees, their limbs choked with moss.

"What the fuck?" Ben yelled, but the old man held his finger to his lips and switched off the radio.

He wiped his face with the sleeve of his red sweatshirt and

fumbled for the bottle of water he'd wedged between the seat and door. He gulped the bottle dry and tossed it into the backseat.

"We'll walk from here," he said.

It sat hunched, a massive home with a caved roof and a hole in its side, rotting furniture and mounds of knickknacks leaking from its guts into the forest. Towering white pillars rose from a crooked front porch, the paint peeled atop graying wood with raised nap from centuries of rain and heat. The house looked to Ben as though it had never been new or clean or beautiful, but had been built as it now stood—a murdered ruin.

"What is this place?" Ben asked.

"An oracle," the old man said. "Only one left I know of."

The old man's foot broke through the porch and he cursed, yanking it free. He knocked on the door twice and stepped back. They waited, bird cries hailing the end of rain.

The door creaked open, and something ancient whispered to them from the dark, "Who's that?"

"An old friend." The old man hitched up his sweatpants and wiped the sweat from his eyes. "I'm in need of information."

"We no longer have information," the voice said.

"I've come with payment."

"Have you come here before?"

"When I was a young man."

The ancient thing stepped into the light and Ben saw an elderly woman, face as wrinkled as sheets balled up at the end of a bed. Her eyes were the color of the winter sky at dusk. She lifted her chin and stared at nothing, reaching out for the old man's face. He took her hand and held it to his cheek, and her fingers crawled like a spider across his nose, dropping down to rest on his chin.

"I remember you," she said. "Lots of cream and lots of sugar."

The old man grinned and then she looked in the direction of Ben.

"And what about him?" She stared with blind eyes. "How does he like his coffee?"

The house was dark, reeking of mold and wet wood. They walked through a labyrinth of high ceilings and cavernous rooms, filled with ornate furniture covered in blossoms of mildew and liquid black trails of ants. The old woman led them past a grand staircase, through a dining room with place settings sitting on a giant table.

They walked through the kitchen and pushed open a heavy creaking door. Two men sat on a couch in a small room with green carpeting and floor-to-ceiling windows dark with grime, remains of old leaves pasted to the outside glass. The two men sat upright, straight and stiff as ship's masts. Both held canes. Both stared blankly with cloud-white eyes.

"Two visitors," the first man said. "Delilah, fetch them some coffee."

"I'm working on it," she said. "Don't bark orders when I'm showing them in."

"I'll do what I want," the first man said. "Get that coffee before I shove this cane up your old cunt."

She muttered something and shuffled away, straining to push through the kitchen door. The old man drew himself up.

"I'm seeking information from another lifetime," the old man said.

The first man patted the wispy white hairs on the side of his head and sniffed proudly. "Name your name."

"Hank Rickey."

The other man nodded and started to talk, but a wet coughing fit overtook him until he spat something thick and bloody onto the floor. "Hank has grown old like us," he said finally. "Time chipped away at him like sand against the Sphinx."

"Still a giant," the first man said. "Heard he led a revival in Jackson some time ago. They said he had a voice that could move mountains."

"True," the other man said.

"Slaughters men like lambs," the first man said. "Marks their blood on the doors of their homes."

"I can't say I believe that," the other man said.

"Makes women throw their underwear," the first man said. "Makes them swear off underwear rest of their lives."

"True," the other man said.

Ben saw tears in the old man's eyes.

"Heard he got diabetes ten years ago," the other man said. "They chopped off his leg at the thigh. No more singing."

"No more singing," the first man repeated.

The other man sniffed. "Heard he left Memphis for Shake. Retirement. Sunday golf, a maid, and a personal chef to help with his blood sugar problems. Wouldn't that be nice?"

"Sure would," the first man said.

The other man nodded. "Took a child bride with him."

"Too much work," the first man said. "Child brides always bitching about one thing or the other."

"They all bitch," the other man said.

The old man asked, "Is the child bride Nadine?"

The first man shrugged. "A child bride is all we know."

Ben looked at the walls. Stock photos in store-bought frames hung high. Cracks ran through the plaster. Cobwebs in the corners billowed gently.

"That all?" the first man said.

The old man rubbed his left pinky. "Last question. My daughter. Is she happy?"

"What daughter is this?" the first man said.

"Lisa Marie."

"Lisa," the other man said.

"Lisa *Marie*," the old man said.

The first man sniffed. "Don't know a Lisa Marie."

The old man stared hard at the floor. He remembered holding her close as if it were yesterday. His baby with tiny clenched fists and eyes that broke his heart. He remembered a dark hotel room, curtains duct-taped with foil on the windows, watching shaky footage of his family emerging from Graceland, pale-faced with grief. *Nothing but bullshit if I stuck around,* he remembered screaming at the television, then he whipped out his snub-nose and popped three into the tube, exploding sparks and the tinkling rush of glass.

He'd read all the true-crime books. He knew what happened to American gods. They'd kidnapped the Lindbergh baby. Everyone clamoring for a piece of divine flesh. For a teaspoon of the muck.

"Lisa Marie is my daughter," the old man insisted, and the first man shrugged and thumped his cane on the floor.

The kitchen door swung open and Delilah shambled in, holding a silver tray upon which sat a silver coffeepot and two chipped porcelain cups. The old man took his cup, nodding at Ben to do the same, and Ben mumbled, "Thank you, ma'am."

The coffee was strong and bitter. The old man heaped a tablespoon of sugar into his and filled it to the top with cream.

"Delilah, bring the knife." The first man moved his head in the direction of the old man. "Now, which one of you will it be?"

"Right here," the old man said.

"What's going on?" Ben asked.

The old man rolled up his sweatshirt sleeve. He exhaled sharply and laughed. He winked at Ben. He kissed his left pinky and Delilah handed him the silver coffee tray, along with a kitchen knife, as he placed his hand flat on the tray.

Ben raised his voice. "What the hell is going on?"

"Payment long overdue," the old man said. "Charlie gave it up twice before, Red once. I never did—always had someone else to bleed for me. Not this time. Not now. Ben, look me in the eye."

He did as the old man said.

"I'll bleed for you," Ben said.

"I know you would," the old man said with a sad smile, and suddenly Ben saw blood pattering on the floor. He saw a pinky, small and silly, sitting all by itself on the silver coffee tray. He saw the knife with a crescent moon of blood clinging to the blade. He saw the two men sitting on the couch smile and thump their canes and the first man asked, "Is it done?" and the old man sighed and said, "Good Lord, yes it is," and then Ben saw nothing.

9.

*B*en awoke in the back of the Caddy as the sun shot low through the forest, creamy orange washed over the pine needles and curled leaves. His shirt stuck to his skin. The back of his head itched, and when he touched it, pain blossomed.

The old man looked over the front seat. He wore his aviators with the missing arm. He grinned. "You fainted like a little girl. Nearly split your skull on the coffee table. But that's okay, because it gave me some time to think."

Ben sat up. He touched the back of his head again and scraped at the hairs, dark grains of blood flaking off. He looked out the window, at the forest. A bird swooped to the ground. It fluttered to a stop and pecked at the dirt.

"We don't have the goods for what needs to be done." The old man held up his bandaged left hand, gauze soaked through with dark red. "I need pain medication. And cash. Plenty of cash. Hank won't give her up for nothing."

Ben searched for something to say. Nothing came to mind except ridiculous questions. He felt displaced, as if half of his body was rooted in a former life—his apartment above Manchurian House, his nostalgia for Jessica, his crazy mom, his ghost of a dad—and here was a new life, a dizzying, dreamlike life, where a beautiful blonde with a scar above her lip had asked him to sleep with her. Where he ate, drank, and fought with bikers. Where blind old men gave prophecy in exchange for pinkies. Where Elvis had never died, but lived in a vinyl-sided box in a Polish suburban neighborhood ten minutes outside of Buffalo.

Ben thought back to the crying boy in the orange shorts. One minute sitting in the sprinkler, holding his knee, tears mixed with sprinkler water, lips trembling. The next minute, eyes still red but now he laughed, back arched, hands overhead. Fingers spread, wedges of blue sky between them. My entrance into this world, Ben thought. Tears to laughter. Pain to pleasure. Just like that. The old man like a light switch. Dark to light. Insane to wise. Just like that.

Ben leaned his head against the window and saw Delilah shuffling down the driveway toward them, carrying a pickling jar.

"The oracle doesn't take money," the old man began, staring out the windshield. "Offer a million and they'd laugh in your face. I've known men paid with their lives to find out why their kids are fucked up or whether their wife ever cheated on them."

Ben laughed quietly. "The oracle. Are you listening to yourself?"

"Course I am."

"You just chopped off your pinky. Doesn't that, I don't know— bother you?"

"If chopping off my pinky means I can find where that sonofabitch took my granddaughter, then I got the better of the deal. It's a pinky, for Christ's sake. What the hell I need a pinky for, at my age?"

"And here comes that crazy lady with a jar. Great. We have three more pinkies between us, so maybe—"

"Calm down, son."

Ben rubbed his face. "The mall wasn't so bad, you know. Or I could've worked at a summer camp. Cute counselors, playing with kids—"

"This is more important. You understand. That's why you came along."

"I came along because I needed the money."

"And because you understand."

"No." Ben shook his head. "I don't understand any of this."

The old man sighed. He stared out the windshield, bandaged hand resting atop the steering wheel. "Never said it was going to be easy. Have faith and follow my lead. I'm a field general in the valley of the strange."

The old man tossed Ben the keys with his good hand, just as Delilah reached the driver's-side window. She held out the jar. Ben saw the pinky floating in yellow liquid.

"I remember how sweet your voice was," she said, her mouth like a hole in a dried apple. "I always found it strange because your voice was so sweet but you were so sad."

The old man took the jar. "I'm still sad, darling. And a little less sweet."

Delilah turned her head in Ben's direction. "How's the boy?"

Ben forced a smile, then stopped because he remembered she couldn't see. "I'm okay."

"He reminds me of you," she said to the old man, and she

shuffled away, dust kicking up in clouds lit yellow by the setting sun. Once she'd disappeared behind the bend of trees, the old man opened the door and set the jar gently on the dirt.

"Those demons would crack her bones and suck out the marrow, they found out I welched," he said.

Ben climbed over the seat and started the car. They pulled from the driveway, driving into the gloaming as the old man sang, *"So long, little pinky. So long."*

Fitchville, Tennessee. Moths collected in the pale of the pharmacy sign and Ben found himself walking under buzzing fluorescent lights, among rows of toothpaste, hemorrhoid creams, shoelaces, and allergy relief. He stopped at the pharmacist's counter, where the old man spoke with a pharmacist named Dean.

Dean shook his head, arms folded across his chest. "I'm sorry, Mr. Barrow, but without a prescription there is nothing I can do for you." He was thin and bald with small eyes hidden behind his wire-rims. His fingernails were freshly manicured.

"Man, look at my hand. I'm dying here."

"Again, I recommend you bring yourself to a hospital, where a doctor will be more than happy to write you a script."

"We don't have the time for all that."

"I'm sorry."

"Sorry don't stop this pain."

"Well, I don't know what you want me to do."

The old man leaned forward. He nodded at the white shelving stocked with pills. "Vicodan. I can see it from here. Fifteen-milligram tabs. You hand me seven of those and we'll be on our way."

"Sir, I cannot do that."

"Generic, then. Not that I trust those goddamn Canadians but—"

"Sir, I cannot do that, and I'm going to have to ask you to leave."

"Leave?"

Dean looked at the old man but found he couldn't match his stare, so he inspected his polished nails. "That's right."

"Ben, get the sack of money from the trunk," the old man said, and he rested his bloodied, bandaged hand on the counter and rolled his three remaining fingers.

Dean sighed. "I will call the police, sir. No amount of money—"

"Just get the goddamn sack, Ben. I'll worry about good old Dean."

Ben shoved through the pharmacy doors. The night was warm. He listened to the crunch of gravel under his sneakers. He jangled the keys in his pocket. The Caddy shone the color of the moon, low and gleaming like a spike of polished bone.

I could leave now, Ben thought. The old man would be safe. Take half of the five grand and keep walking. Leave a note on the dashboard, below the keys. *Sorry, couldn't go on. Keep the rest of the money and good luck finding Nadine.*

Instead he opened the trunk and his cell twittered. He answered without looking at it.

"Ben?"

"Yeah."

"It's Jess."

He saw two shotguns, an AR-15 carbine, and boxes of ammunition lying atop a spare tire. He saw holstered handguns and something that looked like a flak vest.

"What are you doing?" Jess asked.

"I'm standing in a parking lot in Fitchville, Tennessee. Looking at a bunch of guns in the trunk of our 1965 Cadillac."

"You're funny. Are you still with that crazy old man?"

He saw a burlap sack that read *Basmati Rice* on the side, lying next to a hunting rifle with a mounted scope. It was stuffed with crinkled hundreds and twenties.

"Hello?" Jessica asked. "Are you okay? You sound weird."

He leaned back against the rear bumper and closed his eyes, holding his cell with his other hand pressed to his forehead. He thought of a summer day in some park, standing at the top of a hill with his dad. His dad had held him, making his arms into the shape of barrel, and they rolled down, little Ben screaming with laughter and terror.

He thought of the day he discovered he could kill ants. On the driveway where he had stomped them by the dozens, the cement was covered in little black smears. His dad stepped onto the driveway and his bare feet were huge with hair on the toes, and he asked, What are you doing? and Ben answered, Killing ants.

Why would you want to bother those ants? he remembered his dad saying. They have families just like you.

"Ben?"

"I'm here."

Jessica sighed. "I was thinking about us." Her voice pulled through him like barbed wire. "Just old stuff," she continued. "It doesn't feel like any of it happened. Like those seven months—"

"Eight months."

"It's strange but I can't even remember what you look like."

"Like my face is an old photo."

"I guess. So get this: I don't have anything to do tonight because I got into a fight with Alan and then Marcy asked me to go with them to Shooters but I just don't feel—"

"Who's Alan?"

"Don't make me answer that. Can I finish my story?"

Crickets chirped in the hedges lining the parking lot. Ben kept quiet.

"It was a boring story anyway," Jess said.

The old man stalked into the parking lot and tucked his aviators into his sweatshirt pocket. "We're rolling. Take a left out of here and get me to the corner of Elliott and Vine."

Ben said Jessica's name but she was gone.

It was a boring story anyway. His uncle had told him the same thing at his father's funeral, while they stood under the speckled shadow of a giant tree and mourners shuffled past. He'd been reminiscing about a rafting trip taken with Ben's father when they were boys, and halfway through he stopped. *It was a boring story anyway,* his uncle said, squeezing Ben's shoulder with a hand that felt and looked like his father's.

It wasn't true then, Ben thought. And it sure as hell isn't true now.

The bus stop booth on the corner of Elliott and Vine had cracked windows and lighter burns running up the plastic frame. Low-slung storefronts boarded with curled yellowed posters advertised boxing matches of months and years past: Lucky Luziano vs. Enrique Valdemar; The Escobar Kid vs. Ennison Two-Fist Carter; Joe Irish vs. Hampstead Williams. Ben saw another poster, this one more recent. *Elvis Tribute Contest!* it read. *Little Valley, Tennessee. Saturday, June 10. Cash Prizes, Food, Family Fun!*

A girl stood on the corner, leaning against a lamppost. She wore a T-shirt and tight low-rise jeans and she was barefoot with chipped gold nail polish on her toes. The red eye of her cigarette bobbed up and down in the blue-dark.

"Pull over," the old man said. "Sanctimonious prick told me if I needed painkillers, this was the place to go."

He rolled down the window. "Hey, sweet thing," he said, and the girl dropped her cigarette and slinked toward them, slow as a cat on a summer day. She leaned on the windowsill. The scent of smoke and strawberry shampoo filled the car. Her blond hair showed dark roots. She'd plucked her eyebrows too thin. She had narrow eyes and high cheekbones. Ben thought she looked half-Asian.

"Fifty for both," she said. "Condom for everything including blow jobs. I don't touch asses, so don't ask me to put a finger up there."

"What's your name?" the old man asked.

"Ginger."

The old man smiled. "I knew a Ginger once. Long time ago. Get in."

Ben drove aimlessly, pretending as if he knew where to go. Past brick buildings with broken windows and narrow houses with chain-link fences and overgrown lawns. Ginger was younger than Ben first thought, hard-faced with baby fat on her cheeks and heavy makeup particular to hookers, high schoolers, and the women who worked the makeup counter at the Palisade Mall.

"We're not looking for sex," the old man said.

"Well, I don't do nothing weird," Ginger said. "No whips, I mean. Or stepping on your balls or changing your diaper or none of that stuff."

The old man shook his head and held up his bandaged hand.

"I need painkillers. This is a legitimate injury. I lost one of my fingers."

"How'd you do that?"

"Long story," Ben said.

She shrugged and stretched out across the backseat with her bare feet resting on the door. "This is a cool car. Is this like a classic?"

"It is a classic," the old man said. "How long you been selling your body?"

"A month."

"How many men you been with?"

"I don't know. A dozen. Maybe more."

The old man whistled, shaking his head. "Now, I'm going to ask you a personal question, and I don't want you to feel ashamed in front of the young man driving this car. His name is Ben. He's as loyal as they come."

Ben waved hello in the rearview. Then he realized how ridiculous it was, so he gripped the steering wheel and made another turn.

"Did you have sex with all those men?" the old man asked.

"Okay, now you're getting weird." Ginger sat up and wiped the dirt from the bottom of her feet.

Run away, Ben told himself. Back to Cheektowaga. When you get there lock the doors and bar the windows because you know he'll come looking for you. Green aviators, red sweatsuit, and that swept-back hair dyed purple-black. He'll tell you he's on a mission from God. You'll rage against the strip malls, the shrieking boulevards, your dead father, and the stupidity of everyone and everything, but the old man won't care because somewhere in Memphis or Shake or wherever the fuck, there awaits a stripper named Nadine sitting on a throne next to the man who moves mountains with his voice and taught Elvis everything he knew/knows.

"Let me out," Ginger said.

"Keep driving." The old man fished his wallet from his sweat-suit pocket and tossed it to her. "What's in it is yours if you'll answer my questions."

She counted the money and stuffed it in her pocket, then pushed the hair off her face with a certain haughtiness. "What do you want to know?"

"I want to know how many men you've slept with."

"Not many. Most of them only want blow jobs."

The old man frowned. "Do you believe in fate?"

Ginger shrugged.

"Well, I've seen too much to think this universe operates on accident," the old man said. "I put an ad in the paper looking for help, and look what the universe sent me—this young man here. World is full of deviants but Ben is no deviant. Some would chalk it up to luck. Not me. I believe every molecule has its own path—some seek death, others love. Some spend their life in destruction, breaking what the rest of us build like a bully kicking over sand castles. But there are a few men, there are a few, Ginger, that sacrifice themselves for the good of others, and you're looking at two such men. I'm telling you you don't have to hurt anymore. No more shame. No more unspeakable acts that would kill your momma if she ever knew. This is what I'm offering, and if you'll have it, all you gotta do is take my hand."

The old man reached his good hand over the backseat. Ginger's eyes were dark and wide as a doe's.

It's too late for all of us, Ben thought.

Ginger blinked and took the old man's hand. He smiled kindly. "Now," he said, "tell me where I'd find the kind of medication that would help this poor old hand of mine."

* * *

"It doesn't matter if she was drunk. She wouldn't have asked you if she wasn't interested."

"I don't know why I didn't go with her. She was so cool. And really good-looking. Hot, actually. Definitely hot. Hottest girl I've ever talked to. I'm an idiot for not hooking up with her. Do you think I might be depressed?"

"I think you're still caught up in Rebecca."

"You mean Jessica."

"Jessica. Sorry."

Ginger lit a cigarette and offered the first puff to Ben but he shook his head. They sat on the curb outside Lou's Convenience, where the old man told Ben to pull over so he could grab some snacks and use the restroom. Tall boarded buildings stood crooked across the street, weedy lots between them filled with mattresses, rusted shopping carts, and rain-swollen newspapers. The store sign buzzed and flickered red. Moths banged against the neon.

Ben leaned back on his arms and stared at the night sky. "One time I washed Jessica's car while she was at school. Right on the front lawn of my apartment—it was this piece-of-shit LeBaron, but it was a convertible. Her folks bought it for her."

"Were they rich?"

"Sort of, in a suburban, country club way. Anyway, so I picked her up after school and she was grateful, and then we're driving to my place and I put the window down and she freaks out because it wasn't dry and the water was going to leave streaks on the glass."

"What a spoiled bitch."

"But I didn't say anything back. I just apologized. When we got to my place I used my shirt to wipe the glass clean. That's *ridiculous,* isn't it? That's so ridiculous, if my friend told me that story I couldn't be friends with him anymore."

Ginger took another puff. "You're being too hard on yourself. Have you had sex with anyone else since Jessica dumped you?"

Ben rubbed his palms on the warm curb. "No."

"There's your problem."

"The old man said the same thing."

Ginger smiled and exhaled a plume of smoke. Ben looked at her and concocted a fantasy in which he stayed in Fitchville, moving into a grungy studio overlooking a basketball court. From his garret he'd pen poems of urban grit. At night under the lights he'd ball with locals, commiserate with the poor black folk, and flaunt his half-Asian girlfriend/former hooker, who'd sit with her back against the chain link and cheer for her warrior poet.

"Why are you here?" Ben asked.

"In Fitchville?"

"With us. With the old man. When he gave you that speech about molecules and whatever—"

"Like I have better options."

"Do you have a pimp?"

"Uh-huh." She shot smoke from her nose.

"Amazing."

"What's so amazing?"

"I just can't believe you have a *pimp.*"

"I'm a hooker. Hookers have pimps."

"Not all of them."

"How would you know?"

Ben shrugged. "I wouldn't."

"Well, I have a pimp," she said. "And your grandfather didn't seem to care."

"He's not my grandfather."

"Oh. I thought—"

"I answered an ad. I'm his driver."

"I thought he was making that part up. Where are you driving to?"

"A town called Shake. He's looking for his long-lost granddaughter. It's complicated."

"Sounds it."

Ben took the cigarette from Ginger and puffed. "I didn't know what I was going to do this summer," he said. "I was thinking about working at the mall again. You ever work at the mall?"

She smiled a little. "This is my first job."

"That's hilarious. I mean, not—"

"I get it. No offense, right?"

"Right," Ben said. "Anyway. I used to steal ties at my old job. I have a drawer filled with Italian silk ties. Every week I'd roll one up and shove it down my pants. I don't even know why I did it. It was just . . . something to do."

She took the cigarette back. "You don't look like the shoplifting type."

"Oh, yeah. I'm a dangerous man."

They laughed. Then Ben said, "I'm a cheater, too. I cheated on Jessica, with this girl named Carrie. She was anorexic. She had pierced nipples and a red stud in her tongue. Ask me if it was worth it."

"Was it worth it?"

"I'm not sure. We used to fuck in her parents' basement. It had been an apartment for her older brother, so there were all these *Baywatch* posters tacked up over the paneling. Whenever I needed to—you know, not finish?—I would look up at David Hasselhoff."

She nodded. "That would work for me. Is that why Jessica left you? Because of Carrie?"

"Probably. Who knows. We were doomed from the start."

"Why are you telling me all this?"

Ben took the cigarette again. "Making conversation. Trying to paint myself as a neurotic with self-destructive impulses. I don't even smoke, and yet here I am. Puffing away, confessing to theft and infidelity. Is it working?"

"Almost." Ginger looked at him from the side. "So do you want to fuck?"

Ben laughed because he didn't know what else to do.

"If you don't find me attractive, that's all right," she said. "Some guys aren't into the half-Thai thing."

"I'm into the half-Thai thing."

"Would you call me hot?"

"Hot works. Whatever you need me to say, just—"

She ground her cigarette onto the street. "Let's do it in the Caddy. I've always wanted to do it in one of those."

Ben followed her. There was a tattoo of Asian characters on her lower back and she was still barefoot, her heels black with grime.

They maneuvered in the backseat. As she unzipped his pants, Ben wondered if his previous life was still within reach, even if he didn't necessarily want it, and there, he realized, was the source of his depression—the unwillingness to leave what he hated because the alternative, whatever it was, seemed worse.

But not anymore, he thought. Now it had all changed. Now he could stay on the road forever, and he could leave his mom because she was crazy and crazy never got better. It just got crazier. Like the old man. But there was bad crazy and there was good crazy, and the old man had shown Ben there are causes worth fighting for, worth dying for, worth loving for. Either that, Ben thought, or I'm simply thrilled to get laid.

"Make it quick," Ginger said, kissing him between sentences. "I want to finish before the old man gets back. He seems weird about the whole sex thing."

"Do you know who he is?"

She shook her head as Ben slipped her panties down to her knees.

"He's *Elvis*," Ben whispered, and suddenly all was warm and soft. Her stomach was flat and firm and he grabbed her ass. He couldn't believe how little of it there was.

"Like *Elvis* Elvis?" she asked.

He nodded. The seat creaked beneath them. Ginger ground her stomach against his. She bit his neck and clawed his shoulders. Ben closed his eyes. He saw Alex dancing with Heather and Fiona. Sweat dotting her thighs. Daring eyes and her little half-smile.

The car door opened and the old man fell into the passenger seat. Ginger scrambled backward while Ben grabbed his pants and yanked them up. The old man held a sixty-four-ounce plastic cup of Coke and a pouch of beef jerky with a Native American on the front. His speech was slurred.

"What'd you say the name of your pimp was?"

Ginger buttoned her pants. "I didn't." She pulled her shirt down. "His name is Clarence."

The old man went to sip his Coke but missed the straw and it jabbed into his gums. "Tell me about Clarence."

"He's mean."

"Does mean old Clarence have access to the medications I need?"

"Probably."

He licked the blood off his jabbed gum. "Probably like I shouldn't waste my time, or probably like probably?"

"Probably like probably."

"Then tell me where to drive, sugar."

Ginger shook her head. "If he sees me with you, he'll cut off my tits. The last girl tried to leave and he—"

"Uh-huh," the old man mumbled, and he nearly nodded off, eyes flickering shut. Then he roused himself and said, "Ben, when you're finished getting dressed, get the hell up here. We got a meeting with a pimp who fancies himself the Big Bad Wolf."

IO.

Clarence Espino lived in the abandoned mansion of a steel magnate. He preferred to sit alone, on a wooden chair in the middle of his empty living room, imagining flames licking the mansion pillars, the angry townsfolk shouting curses as they thrust their pitchforks and makeshift swords in the air. These were the images he remembered from childhood. He'd watched Technicolor movies with his dad in which Rome burned and barbarians rampaged; one day he thought he, too, would rule a kingdom and watch its decline, because the decay intrigued him. Not the fat times, the glory years, the pax romana, but the end of it all. The corruption and decadence. The diseased whores and conniving senators. The crumbling marble, chipped frescoes, and tales of border outposts overrun.

He'd never imagined success—only fading glory—so when it came, he fought against it. He murdered his friends, scarred his whores, and plunged himself into addiction. He fucked bareback and shared needles with hookers and junkies. One night, while walking home from a poker game, an ambush; Clarence took both barrels from a sawed-off in the gut and chest, and was left bleeding on a street corner.

There, facing the fate he'd wished for since discovering his father dead in his favorite chair with half a face from a self-administered shotgun blast, Clarence asked for mercy. Not because he feared death. Death was his constant companion. He dreamt of it, death by a million causes. Pushed out a fiftieth-floor window, stabbed in the chest, riddled with bullets while waiting at a traffic light. A garrotte slipped around his throat, smooth and silent as a whisper. Bludgeoned with a tire iron, stomped, drowned, burned alive. Death was the only thing in the world Clarence was certain he didn't fear.

He asked for mercy because in that moment when he felt numbness crawling across his face, he realized he'd been death's abandoned twin, left at the world's doorstep and raised to murder the world. And so he awoke three days later, in his bedroom, chest covered in bandages and an IV drip in his arm, one eye blind from six buckshot pellets. He expected rumors of his death to spread through the Fitchville underworld. The jackals would circle. A fitting end, he believed.

Instead they left him alone. For years the people of Fitchville had whispered about the black Lincoln rolling through the streets at night, Clarence at the wheel, windows down, Tech-9 on the seat, hardbangers sitting in the back with AKs. Not anymore. Now he never went out. As his wounds healed, he realized the hardbangers had all left. There was nobody left to fight. Pretending he was dead was easier than pretending he'd ever been alive. He shut himself in, played cards with his whores, read his books, and sat in the wooden chair in the middle of his empty living room. In his solitude Clarence discovered something worse than death: contentment.

* * *

Ben and the old man stood in the empty living room, Clarence in his wooden chair, legs crossed and his face resting in the L of his right hand. Naked women prowled about silently, others sleeping on the floor in a tangle of dark hair and smooth limbs.

"And why should I give her to you?" Clarence asked the old man. "Why should I give anything to you?"

The old man rubbed his eyes and tried to clear his mouth, but he'd taken too many blue pills. He knew he didn't sound his best. Like a foolish old man, he thought. Goddammit, when this girl needs your help, you're no better than anyone else in her wasted life. Remember singing lullabies to Lisa Marie when you couldn't stay awake with drool leaking down your chin like some fucking retard?

"I remember," the old man said. He hadn't meant to speak but the words came out anyway. He swayed and Ben caught him by the arm.

The old man looked at Ben and wished he had a million dollars to give. In his prime he'd known a dozen men who'd take a bullet for him, but not one when he was just a poor kid. Known a dozen men who called him faggot and white nigger, but not one who'd hold him upright when his strength failed.

"What he's trying to say—" Ben began but Clarence held up his hand.

"I'm not talking to you," Clarence said. "I'm talking to that old junkie in the ratty clothes. The old junkie who wants me to give up my favorite girl on account of her pitiful life, who thinks he can do better for her."

"Better than what she has now," the old man said. "I'm offering her a chance to do something righteous."

Clarence laughed. "Only righteous thing that girl does is suck a good dick. So get your dick sucked good and bring that bitch back here before I lose patience."

"God sent her to me," the old man said. "When He's finished, He'll send her back." Then he took out his wallet and waved it in the air. "There's also the matter of medication Ginger said you'd be happy to sell."

Clarence laughed again and sat up with his hands resting on his knees. He looked at the old man wearing his red sweatsuit with his finger-combed hair, and there was something familiar about him, like a McDonald's sign or the taste of a Twinkie.

"Do I know you?" Clarence asked.

The old man stumbled forward and dropped his wallet. He slipped from Ben's grasp and fell, splitting his lip on the floor.

Clarence gestured to one of his women. She stretched her arms overhead, slowly, and retrieved the wallet. Ben could smell her perfume as she walked away.

The old man touched his bleeding lip and smiled at Ben.

"Your five thousand is in that wallet," the old man said. "The rest is all gone. Faster than I thought."

Clarence stared at the three of them. The old man looked like he was on the verge of collapse but it didn't seem to matter. Nothing seemed to matter to the old man, except for whatever had pulled him out of seclusion. For a moment Clarence wanted to join the old man like Ginger and this cocksure boy who was too naive to know how close they all were to getting killed, right there in his living room. It must be something special, Clarence thought, if they're willing to go through all this. I've never been a part of something special. Granted, I've never wanted to, but maybe that's just sour grapes.

"Five thousand gets you safe passage out of this town," Clarence said. "Another five gets you the medication, and I'll throw in the bitch for nothing. Consider her a gift. From one fallen king to another."

They drove through the night until the sun washed over the hood of the Caddy. The old man told Ben to stop at the next motel. In separate rooms they slept, the old man in his clothes atop the blankets, sweat washing the coating off pills he clenched like a baby with a rattle. He slept with the lights on because he hated waking up in the dark; the television blared past the twelve o'clock news and into daytime soaps, its music filling his dreams and making his nightmares melodramatic. In one dream he stood on a dark stage and the audience stood shoulder to shoulder, all faceless clones who stayed silent no matter how loud he sang or whether his favorite gospel numbers moved him to tears. He knew they were hungry and his singing could only feed them for so long. When he lost his voice he began to peel off strips of his own flesh, tossing it to them, watching them smear their sharp-toothed mouths with his blood. On it went until he couldn't peel anymore and then they began to ascend the stage, clawing up the risers, mouths chomping.

Ben slept with Ginger in the other room, both of them clothed under a sheet. Ginger slept with her head in the crook of Ben's arm. Before he drifted off he realized the last girl to sleep in his arms was Jessica, and she'd smelled different from Ginger. Jessica smelled like the mall, cocoa butter, and raspberry lip gloss. Ginger smelled like cigarettes and the back of an old car.

He'd bought her—it was a blunt way to see it, but he couldn't see it any other way—with the five thousand the old man had given him. All this time he'd worried about his skin, his jokes, his lack of muscled arms, when the solution had been cash. Just buy a girlfriend. Tack on the monthly payments as you would a mortgage or car loan.

He wondered if there was decent work in whatever town they were now in. Something where he could sweat out his anxieties and afford a small home and a small life. He didn't need travel; he imagined Ginger wouldn't need it, either, because small-town hookers weren't the jet-setting type.

And he'd tell Jessica, of course. Talk about his new life and suddenly he's a hundred years older than her freshman lap dogs. Maybe she'd even visit—he imagined a dinner with Ginger and Jessica, Ginger dressed in something short and tight, coiling a smooth, taut leg around his leg, fork-feeding him ziti spears while Jessica stares at them over the rim of her wineglass—and the day of their breakup when he asked Mindy to dinner would seem like nothing more than a player being a player. Every stupid thing he'd done would make sense. Failings transformed into charming idiosyncrasies, moral errors a necessary consequence of the life of a sex-starved cad.

Ben had tried those explanations before, after the affair with Carrie. Carrie the anorexic. Carrie the sort-of-goth chick. Chopped black hair, five percent body fat, a victim of sexual abuse who fucked like a berserker, leaving claw marks down his back and purple marks on his shoulders; she'd threatened him with lesbian affairs but never made good, dumped him on Valentine's Day, and fucked him later that week in her parents' basement. He'd known Carrie before Jessica, having met her in a sociology class. In the beginning, when he hadn't yet fallen into the all-encompassing tailspin of a love affair with a seventeen-year-old blond Lolita, sex with Carrie was therapy with a side of orgasm; she hadn't been freaked out by his dad's death. When he started dating Jessica a month after the funeral, he no longer needed Carrie but he couldn't stop.

There's a whole culture built around sadness, Alex had said. *It makes you feel like a part of something bigger.*

He got caught—one morning Jessica dropped by unannounced as Carrie was leaving—and he begged Jessica for forgiveness. He never saw Carrie again, but the spell was broken. His infallibility shattered, the only chance he had at keeping Jessica. Either worship or nothing, he realized.

Ben awoke in the motel room, sweating. He stared down at Ginger's little head tucked in the crook of his arm. Drawn curtains framed in sunlight. The weak air-conditioning whirred. He moved his arm and she tilted her head up.

"Is it tomorrow?"

He checked the clock radio. "It's almost five."

"We should stay here." She yawned. "I just want to sleep and eat. Eggs, toast, extra-crispy hash browns. Ask your grandpa if we can stay."

"He's not my grandpa."

"I know, I know. But I don't know what else to call him."

"Elvis."

She laughed a little. "I've never seen anyone handle Clarence the way he did."

"He's good like that. You know he's got an arsenal in the trunk."

She looked up at him. "For real?"

Ben nodded.

"What's he need it for?"

"Hank Rickey."

"Who's Hank Rickey?"

Ben pulled himself out from under Ginger and sat on the edge of the bed. He yawned and ruffled his hair. The brown carpet felt stiff against his bare feet. "Hank Rickey took the old man's granddaughter."

"You mean Elvis."

"That's right. Elvis."

Then he shuffled to the bathroom and looked at himself in the mirror under the green fluorescent light. He splashed cold water on his face, letting it drip while he watched Ginger in the mirror's reflection, her lithe body stretched on the bed. She put her hands behind her head, staring at the ceiling as if it were the sky on a summer afternoon.

"He sure took a lot of those pills," Ginger said. "My mom used to take pills. She said it was for panic attacks."

Ben fell into the easy chair pushed against the wall. He stared at Ginger.

"What?" she said.

"Nothing."

"You don't look like it's nothing."

"I dreamt about my dad this morning."

"So."

"So he died last year and I haven't dreamt about him in a long time."

"Oh shit." She frowned. "I'm sorry. What was the dream about?"

"Dreams always sound stupid when you tell people what happened."

Ginger flipped onto her stomach and rested her chin on her

hands. "I don't care. I like hearing other people's dreams because I never dream."

"Everyone dreams. You just don't remember them."

"Same difference. So tell me."

Ben told her his dream. When he finished he stared at the brown carpet and remembered yelling at his mom a month after the funeral because his dad's mud-caked sneakers were still in the foyer, sitting in the corner atop a yellowed sheet of newspaper dotted with dried mud.

His mom had stood at the kitchen sink with her graying hair pulled back tight. She was barefoot. Through the small window above the sink Ben saw the cloud-darkened sky.

"Let me make you a sandwich," she said. "Would you like a sandwich?"

"Throw those sneakers away, Mom. They're useless."

"I will. But you have to eat. You don't look well."

It was summer break and two months earlier his dad asked him to hose off his sneakers because he'd gotten them dirty while unclogging the drain tile in their backyard. Every day he reminded Ben and every day Ben forgot. One month later he was dead, yet there they remained, blue-and-white Nikes, encased in cracked mud, still smelling of his dad's feet.

"I'm not hungry," Ben said. "Don't change the subject."

She turned to him, and Ben realized how old she looked. The way the freckled skin on her neck crinkled like crepe paper. The way her bones showed through her clothes.

"Please don't touch them," she said.

"But he doesn't need them anymore."

"I know," she said. She looked like she could scream; all he could do was walk away before he screamed, too.

One year had passed and whenever Ben came home to visit they were still there: blue-and-white Nikes, laces frozen in mud. Soon they moved to the closet, where he figured they remained, buried under forgotten gloves, hats, and winter scarves.

He stared at the motel room ceiling and pushed his sadness down to wherever it was supposed to be. It had been one year and he felt that was long enough. They build skyscrapers in a year, he thought. And airports and suburban developments. Get over it. Move on.

Ginger pulled off her shirt. She giggled and flung herself back, bouncing off the mattress. She pulled the sheet to her chin, grinning. Her lips were very red, her teeth very white. A clump of mascara clung to the tip of her eyelash.

"Let's fuck," she said.

Ben leapt onto the bed and she screamed with laughter.

II.

They knocked on the old man's door after sunset and when he didn't answer Ben walked in. The lights were off but the TV was on. In the flickering dark Ben saw the old man lying on the motel bathroom floor, head propped against the wall, spilled complimentary mouthwash in a green puddle, bath towel clutched in one hand. Dried vomit crusted to the side of his face, and his red sweatpants smelled of urine. When Ben touched his shoulder he opened one eye and started to sing.

"TodayIstumbledfrombedwiththundercrashinginmyhead."

Nine P.M. Shelby Hospital waiting room. Nubby orange office chairs and coughing children. Ginger slept with her head on Ben's shoulder as he checked his voice mail. The Elvis biography sat in his lap.

Benny boy, where the fuck are you? Call me. My name is Steve and we used to play basketball together.

Hi, it's Samantha. I'm driving home from work and I was going to stop for a beer at Jack Astor's if you were around, but I guess you're not, so bye-bye.

Ben. Rent is due. Call me.

It's Jess. Listen, I'm going to be back home only for a week and I wanted to know if we could meet for some coffee. I'll be in my room all night unless Alan comes over. Call me before you go to bed.

Ben saw the doctor walking toward them. He nudged Ginger awake.

The doctor squirted a dollop of Purel into his palm and rubbed his hands together. He forced a smile at Ben, wrinkled his forehead at Ginger, and put his hands on his hips. "Your grandfather is resting comfortably," he said. "His pinky, though—it's infected. Can you tell me how he lost it?"

"He slammed it in a car door," Ben said.

"He must have slammed it pretty hard."

"You should've heard the scream."

"I bet." The doctor raised his eyebrows as if he didn't quite believe Ben but was willing to let it slide. "Anyway, we cleaned it and I have him on Cipro for ten days. As to the overdose, we found these." He held up an orange pill bottle. "Which we believe he purchased in Canada. Made any trips to Canada recently?"

"No."

"Then I'd keep an eye on his Internet use. Most seniors mail-order nowadays. It's a wonder we don't see more cases like this." He handed Ben a white slip of paper. "This is a prescription for Percocet. Not as heavy as what your grandfather was taking, but still, keep the bottle on your person so this doesn't happen again."

"Can we see him?"

"Sure. He's groggy, so it might take a little song and dance to get his attention."

Ben thanked the doctor and they started to walk away, but the doctor cleared his throat.

"You should know your grandfather's exhibiting signs of dementia."

"Like Alzheimer's?" Ben asked.

The doctor plucked a clipboard off the intake counter and glanced at a chart, whistling quietly through his teeth. "It appears to be in the early stages. Of course we'd need to run some tests before saying anything definitive."

"So it is Alzheimer's?"

"The best we can do at this point is make an educated guess. But his behavior indicates some sort of impairment. The pinky accident may point to a loss of motor ability. . . . Tell me, is his whole Elvis getup a personal preference?"

"He loves Elvis," Ben said.

"I got that. He called for his daughter before we inserted the stomach pump."

"Lisa Marie?"

The doctor cocked an eyebrow. "Who else?"

The old man's room was small but private. The vertical blinds were pulled tight. A small TV hung in the corner of the ceiling.

The old man stared at Ben with unfocused eyes and tried to sit up. His hand was wrapped in fresh gauze. "*Mercenaries*," he whispered. "Before we hit Shake, we need mercenaries. Many as we can afford."

Ginger touched the old man's hand and he smiled, so she kept it there. His green aviators sat on a small table near the bed. The single lamp burned dim.

"How are you feeling?" Ginger said.

"Tired," the old man said. "Told the doctor I'm on four hundred milligrams Lortab every three hours, just like the *PDR* says. I've been off Nardil for a month, so he doesn't need to worry about contraindications. He took my pills anyway, even though I told him four hundred milligrams Lortab every four hours. Just like the *PDR* says."

"I don't think we can make it to Shake," Ben said.

"We have to."

"I checked your rice sack and there's fifty bucks left. We don't have any money. We barely have enough to get back to Cheektowaga."

The old man tried to shout but a wad of mucus foiled his plans and he launched into a wet coughing fit. Ginger poured him a cup of water.

"Nadine needs me." He breathed hard. "A life with Hank isn't any sort of life. That's why I hired you. That's why I stepped back into the world I left behind—"

Ben held up his hand. "Does Nadine even exist?"

The old man paused with his cup in midair. "Sugar, get my wallet from the nightstand drawer."

She found it next to an empty pack of chewing gum and a dog-eared copy of *The Essential Kabbalah*.

"Behind my Wegmans Shoppers Club Card there's a photo," the old man said.

She took it out and handed it to Ben. A black woman held an infant, tiny wrinkled face captured in mid-cry.

"Nadine Emma Brown," the old man said. "Emma sent me that photo two months before she died of heart failure."

Ben handed it back but the old man shook his head. "You're holding redemption right there. Keep it as a reminder."

"I can't get an apartment in Amsterdam with redemption," Ben said.

"What do you need an apartment in Amsterdam for anyway?" the old man said. "The French are assholes. Christ's sake, they think Grace Jones is a genius."

Ben stared at the photo. "We need money."

"Then find money."

"I have two hundred bucks in my account."

"I don't even have an account," Ginger said.

The old man squeezed his eyes shut and tried to order his thoughts. Think. Think of something.

Jet rides and round beds covered in purple velvet. Those sweet twins in their little pink panties giving him a rubdown after that show in Buffalo. Then there was the time he and Lamar broke into the Embassy Hotel kitchen and ate an entire twenty-four-pack of kosher dogs. Washed it down with a handful of ludes and spent the next day puking up processed meat.

Used to be he needed money and one tour sufficed. Three hundred thousand a week in 1973. Money always in his pocket. Grab a thick fold and yank it out. Fifties. Hundreds. Stack of dead presidents six feet high. Unfathomable now. Made his living selling memorabilia on eBay. One thousand for a signed scarf. Two hundred for a backstage pass.

Then he remembered the poster.

Elvis Tribute Contest!
Little Valley, Tennessee. Saturday, June 10
Cash Prizes, Food, Family Fun!

"I got an idea," the old man said. "But first get me in the shower."

He made Ben stand in the bathroom while he showered, standing in his soaked red sweatsuit with his eyes shut, water pattering against the velvety nap like rain on moss. His bandaged hand soaked through and blood dripped from the gauze, snaking down the drain in a winding tendril.

"It's two hours to Little Valley," the old man said. "Hundred bucks should get us a room for the night. Tomorrow I'll clean up, enter that contest and do my thing. Then with cash prize in hand, we'll head off to Shake and take care of business."

"What about clothes?" Ben asked. "Don't you need an outfit of some kind?"

"One-fifty should get us a decent pair of slacks, decent shirt, decent shoes, and decent belt repair. I'll have them sew up my lion's head buckle. Sight of that sonofabitch alone should land first prize."

He soaped his armpits through the red sweatshirt and spit water like a Greek fountain. Then he laughed and spit again, and Ben thought about Ginger squeezing his hand when the doctor said dementia.

Ben sorted through the clothing racks, the scrape of hangers on metal rails reminding him of school shopping with his mom. He shifted his cell to his other ear.

"We're going to the Allentown Art Festival tomorrow," Patrick said. "Eric's meeting us at Pano's and we'll probably walk there."

"I can't make it."

"Art chicks, Ben. Easy art chicks as far as the eye can see. Nothing but nipples and pierced belly buttons."

Ben lifted a pair of pants and held them up for Ginger, who shook her head. "Sorry, man," Ben said. "I won't be home until next week."

"Where are you?" Patrick said.

"At a Wal-Mart in Tennessee."

"Awesome. Are you shopping?"

"Uh-huh."

"For the old man?"

"Who else."

"What happened to Memphis?"

"Long story." Ben lifted another pair of pants, and again Ginger shook her head.

"Do you still think he's Elvis?" Patrick said.

"Get serious," Ben said. "I'm not an idiot."

"What about that hot girl who wanted to fuck? You said no, which is something only an idiot—"

Ben winked at Ginger and she stuck out her ass and slapped it. "I got someone else," he said.

"Let me say hi," Ginger said, and Ben tossed her the phone.

"Hello? Is this Patrick?"

"Yeah, this is Patrick. Who's this?"

"Ginger."

"Well, hello, Ginger. Are you Ben's new girlfriend?"

"No. Ben's my new pimp."

"Excuse me?"

Ben went to grab the phone but Ginger pulled away. "You heard me," she said. "Pimp. P-I-M-P."

Patrick laughed. "Pimp as in hookers and pimps, or pimp as in hip-hop parlance—"

"Pimp as in a man who owns my ass and rents it out."

"You're *serious*," Patrick said.

"Totally. Ben bought me from my old pimp. Clarence. Dude had one eye."

"Let me talk to Ben."

"Don't you like talking to me?"

Ben grabbed Ginger's arm and pulled her close. With his other hand he grabbed his cell but she kept listening, rising up on her toes and craning her neck.

"I do like talking to you," Patrick said. "But this is just fucking unbeliev—"

Ben closed the cell. It twittered moments later. He stuffed it in his pocket and kissed Ginger long and hard. They stood in the middle of the men's clothing aisle, under high fluorescent lights with Muzak playing "Burning Love."

When they gave the old man the pants they'd chosen, he slung them over his shoulder and gazed across the store, eyes narrowed, mouth tight. "You got good taste," he said. "I'm going to find a pair of boots. Think you could get me a shirt with a dragon on it? Or any kind of predator? Something powerful. Like a lion or tiger."

"What about an elephant?" Ginger said. "They're powerful."

"They're not a predator."

"And a dragon is?"

"Sure."

"What do they eat, then?"

The old man thought for a moment. "People, I guess. Ben?"

"People," Ben said.

Ginger and Ben searched the racks for a shirt, and she told him stories about her childhood—how she'd lived with her mom in a small town in Wisconsin, in her grandparents' farmhouse with a rickety porch and grapevines curled up the siding. There were only one hundred students in her elementary school, ice-cream cones only cost a dollar, and the town doctor wore a hat and bow tie. Ben thought the sound track to her childhood should've been the music that played during those "Beef, it's what's for dinner" commercials with Sam Elliot sounding like his throat was stuffed with gravel and you could almost hear the bristles of his mustache scratching against the studio mic.

Ginger said she'd never known her father, and a succession of her mother's boyfriends always hurt them both in some way. Some were drunks, some were meth fiends, some touched Ginger when she was a little girl, and even though she squeezed her legs shut they touched her anyway. There was one, Ginger said, the most normal of the bunch, who carried a Bible and spoke of Jesus and forgiveness, until Ginger came home early from school and found him in the living room standing behind her friend Susan's dad with his suit pants down around his ankles and the TV showing Matthew Modine's *E! True Hollywood Story*.

Then there was the year of panic attacks, her mother holed up in her room with a box of tissues, a mumbling TV, and a steady supply of pills. Ginger said she'd tried the pills a few times but they made her dizzy and gave her nightmares, and the one time she came to school high, the teacher called child services. Soon after that her mother started dating the child services investigations worker.

Ben didn't believe Ginger's stories but he didn't care because the telling of stories had always been his favorite part. Sometimes he wished for a new girlfriend just so he could hear new stories and tell his own stories to fresh ears. It was like the slow unveiling of a painting, slipping off the white sheet inch by inch and discovering every new brush stroke and splash of color. He'd honed his own stories for maximum effect—the dramatic pauses, the ironic twists, the hand-to-your-mouth betrayals and sly admissions of bedroom prowess mixed in with self-deprecating asides of neuroses and obsessions. In his tales he was the perfect rogue, a victim of self-destruction and poor judgment, but there was potential in there, his stories promised, if only he could find the right woman.

And while he knew Ginger wasn't that woman—he couldn't imagine bringing her home, with her mid-nineties-style tight jeans and overdone makeup and possibly fucked-up childhood—he was content to pretend for a little while. One week ago he'd been contemplating a retail job, a drive to visit Jessica at college, and his Amsterdam fantasy. None of them were particularly realistic. None of them were close to what he had going on now—shopping for Elvis clothes with a hooker in a twenty-four-hour Wal-Mart.

If this isn't anthropology, Ben thought, I don't know what is.

They found a silky button-down shirt with a rattlesnake sewn over the breast. A desert landscape printed on the back showed a milky blue moon high above a mountain ridge. They brought it to the old man, who sat in the shoe aisle on a small stool and labored to squeeze his foot into a shiny black boot. Sweat dripped from his high forehead, making dark spots on his red sweatpants. Shoppers shuffled past, zombie eyes staring straight ahead.

Ben held up the shirt.

"That a rattler?" the old man said.

"It is."

"I like it, man. Kinda looks like a small dragon. What do you think of these boots?"

Ben nodded. "Shiny."

"I like the heels," Ginger said.

In the checkout line the old woman working the register did a double take, life flaring into her tired eyes. Her hair was blue, the same shade as her Wal-Mart apron. She wore rose-colored glasses, thick as windshields.

She scanned the first item. *Silky button-down. Bad to the Bone collection.*

"Looks like you're going to that tribute contest," she said.

The old man nodded. "Yes, ma'am."

"Aren't you a little old?"

"I'm a lot old."

"You sort of look like him," she said. "If he'd made it out of Graceland alive."

She scanned the second item. *White poly slacks. Elasti-comfort waistband.*

"I remember when Elvis first came out," she said, grabbing the boots. "My parents were scared of him. What he did with those hips . . ."

E-Z Slide gaucho boots. Genuine Leatherine.

"Then he went to the Army. Cut off that gorgeous hair and took the rebel right out of him, like Delilah did with Samson. He wasn't the same after that with all those silly movies." She shook her head and counted the cash. "It only got worse from there. The gospel songs, the Vegas years. And the way he treated his wife." She pursed her lips and folded the pants. "I never understood what she saw in him. A pretty woman like that, putting up with all his cheating and drug abuse. I tell you what *I* would have done—"

"Not a goddamn thing," the old man said.

The old woman looked up. "Excuse me?"

"You heard me," the old man said. Ben shot Ginger a worried look and he gently took the old man's arm.

"We really should get to the hotel—"

"You wouldn't've done a goddamn *thing*," the old man said. "You don't think Priscilla had her own toys to play with? You don't think she made secret phone calls and told me she was going to lunch when she was really lying on her back while some GOD-DAMN HANGER-ON LAID PIPE?"

"Priscilla was a faithful wife!" the old woman shouted. "Everything I read—"

The old man pounded his fist on the counter. "*Lies*. Every one of them. Gossip rags and traitors threw me into the fire. Made me into the *bad guy*. Fuck them, and fuck you for believing it."

Shoppers turned and stared. Out of the corner of his eye Ben saw a tall, heavy man lumbering toward them, dressed in white short-sleeve shirt and tie. His Wal-Mart name tag read *Bill Sawyers, Manager*.

"This gentleman cursed at me," the old woman said. Her voice shook and Ben saw spittle collecting in the corners of her mouth. "He cursed at me and physically intimidated me—"

The old man hammered the counter with his fist again. He didn't like the way it sounded, so he hammered it once more. "She's goddamn right I cursed at her. Nosy old cooze sticking her business where it isn't welcome. Don't say a goddamn word, Bill Sawyers. Thirty years ago I'd have my boys haul your fat ass in the parking lot and whip you like a rented mule—"

Bill Sawyers put his hands on his hips. "Sir, there's no reason for threats. Now, if you've already purchased your items . . ."

"It's not his fault," Ginger said, stuffing the black boots into a bag. "Everything was fine until this cranky bitch started talking smack."

The old woman put her hand to her chest. "Excuse me?"

"Oh, don't act all proper like nobody ever called you bitch before."

"Sir, if you've already purchased your items, I'm going to ask you all to leave. I don't want any trouble but—"

"Then tell that cranky bitch to keep her mouth shut." Ginger glared at the old woman. "Go on and say something. I'll knock your dentures the fuck *out*."

Ben stepped between Ginger and the old woman. The old woman yelled. Ginger yelled back. Bill Sawyers raised his voice.

The old man slung the bag over his shoulder. He looked around the store, at the people who stared. Hazy memories of every place he'd ever been. Jackson. Montgomery. Austin. Vegas. *Vegas.* Like a sponge that sucked everything in and wrung it out dirty. Last bastion of the irrelevant. Corporatized freak show. Dress it up however you want, drizzle it with sex appeal and a heartbreaking tremolo, but it's always been about the freak show. Suddenly he longed for the dark of his Cheektowaga home. The quiet of his side street in the winter. Snow plowed into dirty mountains, anorexic trees, and *Baywatch* reruns.

Remember Nadine, he told himself. It's about Nadine. All that matters.

The old man pulled Ginger away and Ben stayed behind, apologizing to the old woman and apologizing to Bill Sawyers, Bill nodding as if he understood that these sorts of things happen with delusional old men.

As they walked through the automatic doors, the old man took a deep breath. "You tell them I was sorry?"

Ben nodded.

"Good. Sometimes I forget my place. I don't ever mean to be angry."

The night air was cool and damp, and the quiet of the bare parking lot sounded nice. The old man realized he couldn't remember what kind of car he owned. Might be a wisteria-on-white Caddy, he thought. Then again, it might not.

hey spent Friday night in a ground-level room at the Take 5 Motel, an engine idling outside the front windows. The Denny's restaurant sign glowed across the parking lot. Ginger lay asleep in bed and the old man had pulled out the couch, Ben fitting the sheets while the old man tucked the corners of a blanket under the thin mattress. Then the old man sat on a cushy chair in the corner, feet flat on the dark green carpet with legs apart, hands on the armrest. He was slightly stoned from the Percocet and a couple tabs of codeine he kept in his pocket. That old feeling of floating felt good, warm and easy like a bath on a summer night.

Ben and the old man played cards for an hour. Casino and War. Ben couldn't believe how excited the old man got when it was time for War. *One*—he'd say, laying down the first card. *Two*—he'd say a little louder, laying down the second card. Then he'd hold up the third card, foot tapping on the floor, and he'd turn it over and shout *Three!* and it didn't matter who won because he laughed every time.

It rolled past two and Ben got tired but the old man insisted he stay up with him and tell him stories about his childhood.

"That's funny," Ben said.

"What's funny?"

"You wanting to hear anything about my childhood."

The old man smiled, slowly. "The money's all gone but you stayed. I can't think of one person in my previous life half as loyal."

"Loyal," Ben said. He lay back on the couch bed, staring at the ceiling. "I think I'm still here because I don't want to go back."

"Then don't. Keep running."

"Like you?"

"I didn't run." The old man closed his eyes. "I became a ghost. Now, come on—tell me what you were like as a boy. And don't leave nothing out."

Ben talked until three, the old man's eyes occasionally fluttering shut, but every time Ben stopped talking, he mumbled for him to keep going. So he told the old man everything. Details he'd forgotten about his first kiss (she wore a yellow blouse with buttons shaped like monkeys), about his first fight (the headlock and basketball-chucking incident), and the phone call from his uncle, the day his father died (*Benjamin, are you sitting down and are you somewhere safe?*).

The old man's eyes were closed and his chest slowly moved up and down as if he were asleep. Ben thought maybe he was. He sat up and the springs creaked. The old man jerked awake and licked a spit bubble off his lip. He stared at Ben.

"How long your daddy been dead?" he said.

"One year."

"Been almost fifty years since my momma died. Sunday nights . . . whew. Still hard. You dream about him?"

"Sometimes. My mom dreams about him every night. She still talks to him."

"I still talk to Jesse."

"Your twin brother?"

The old man nodded. "He died a long time ago. Age of the dinosaurs."

"But when you talk to him it's more like talking to yourself. You don't think he can actually hear—"

"Sure I do."

"That's crazy."

"Sure is."

Ben bit his thumbnail. He thought if he could trade sanity for believing his father had transcended death, he just might do it. Not only would it mean his father never died, but it would give him his own sense of immortality. Death was his greatest, most enduring fear. Death made him desperate. For a girlfriend, for money, for direction. He lived in constant awareness that he had only so much time, even less if he included bad luck. The promise of immortality would mean no more desperation. He could take his time. He could wander, aimlessly, without guilt.

Suddenly it made sense. His mom speaking with his dad in her dreams; the commuters who gripped their steering wheels and buzzed past his apartment building every morning; the Palisade Mall walkers in their gleaming white sneakers, fat asses waddling in time with their flabby arms; the annoying women in their Home Shopping Network suits who clipped coupons and waited outside the front gates of Harold's to get their husbands two-for-one Italian silk ties. It was all a battle against desperation. You could drink yourself silly and smoke ten bowls of high-grade skunk, you could shop, you could obsess over ex-girlfriends, or you could go crazy. Let your mind decay. Believe your dead twin brother was listening from the grave.

And Ben realized he couldn't do it. It was too late. His last enduring fantasy had been as a boy, when he believed his father was the gateway to a giant world. Behind his father lay oceans swimming with monsters, and empires with kings who sat in their mountain halls, and exotic women dancing with veils covering half their face. His father as big as the moon, and behind him a world bigger than anything he ever knew.

But grief had shrunk the world to something he could fit in his pocket; now this old man had taken it out and replaced it with his own tiny world.

"You have to accept that your brother is gone," Ben said. "If you don't, you can't process what happened."

"Sounds pretty smart," the old man said.

"It's closure."

The old man frowned, eyes shut. "Closure is bullshit. Life goes on and that's good enough. Your momma needs to talk to her dead husband, who are we to say he don't talk back?"

"Does Jesse talk back?"

The old man thought for a moment. He opened his eyes and struggled to focus on the young man sitting on the edge of the couch bed.

"No," the old man said. "But that don't mean he can't hear me."

It was bright as two suns the next morning, a clear sky the color of a Miami swimming pool, cars thrumming past the Take 5 Motel while Mexicans trimmed hedges lining the parking lot. The noise roused the old man, who found himself in his cushy chair with a stiff neck and dry mouth. Sheets lay in a ball at the edge of the bed. The room smelled like a shower. He found the bathroom lights on, and sprinkles of foundation powder in the sink.

He grabbed the clock radio and held it up because he couldn't find his glasses: 11:33. He saw the little half-Asian girl had ironed his clothes and laid them out on the couch bed.

The old man lurched into Denny's, dressed in a motel bathrobe, freshly shaven with his hair combed back and dots of toilet paper lining a constellation across his neck. He wore a new pair of brown-tinted aviators he'd bought from a sunglass kiosk in the plaza across from the motel.

Ben and Ginger sat in a booth, finishing their breakfast. They spotted him and waved him over.

Ben laughed. "Jesus, look at him."

"He's a fucking god," Ginger said.

The young Mexican woman behind the register stared at the old man's bathrobe and slippered feet.

"Sir, I don't know if you can wear that in here."

He grinned. "I got a big show today and I don't want to get food on my new clothes."

"But I don't know if you can wear that in here."

"Course I can. Beautiful women are sympathetic. So what do you say?"

She bit her lower lip, then smiled a little and grabbed a menu. The old man led her to the booth and squeezed himself next to Ginger.

"Cheese omelet and eight strips bacon." The old man pushed away the menu. "Darling, make that bacon nice and crispy. I like it when it crumbles."

Ben told the old man he'd gotten the particulars—the contest was being held in the Little Valley Convention Center. Two P.M. start. Thirty-dollar entry fee, five-thousand-dollar first-place cash prize. Two categories: Sun Records Elvis and Aloha from Hawaii Elvis. The woman on the phone told Ben there'd been a third category last year—Vegas Elvis—but no one could tell the difference between Aloha from Hawaii Elvis and Vegas Elvis.

The old man listened as best he could. He still hadn't found his prescription glasses and everything was blurry—the fat kid and his girlfriend eating at the next table over, the manager wandering down the rows, eyes darting from table to table. His pinky throbbed and he had to take a shit, and the idea of doing anything other than sleeping in a dark motel room suddenly filled him with dread.

Nadine, he thought. Remember Nadine.

The old man bit into a piece of bacon. "Five thousand isn't much but it'll have to do. We finish by six, we should be at Hank's before sunset."

"Where does he live?" Ben said.

The old man took another bite. "Hank's family got a big house in Redstone Ridge. Last time I saw him, he told me was going to take care of his sick momma. Almost fifty years ago. Now, does time fucking move or does time fucking move?"

Then he stood and bent forward until his back cracked, and he dropped a crinkled twenty on the table. "I'm going to get ready. Give me an hour alone."

Storm clouds swept in, carried on winds that blew hedge trimmings across the motel parking lot, lifting straw wrappers and Styrofoam clamshells from the Denny's Dumpster. The motel manager told Ben it was the ghost of Elvis—every year it rains during the tribute contest, he said. No matter how sunny the day of, a storm blows in like something out of the Bible.

Ginger tried running on the treadmill in the motel exercise room, watching Jerry Springer on the television mounted high in the corner above a water cooler. Ben knocked on their room door and knocked again, then he opened it, bracing for the worst—the old man in a puddle of puke and piss, eyes bulging and lips blue, empty pill bottle cupped in his cooling hand. Instead he found him sitting in the cushy chair in the corner with the shades drawn, dressed in his underwear.

Slivers of light banded the old man's face; dark forehead, blue-gray nose, dark mouth, blue-gray chin. In his lap Ben saw a shotgun, long and lean. Rain began its tap against the windows. Thunder grumbled softly.

"Old boxers never lose power," the old man said. He sounded like he was speaking in slow motion. "They don't have the speed anymore, so they learn misdirection. That's what Hank told me. Make their opponent watch the paunch jiggle and wiggle, then *bam*, hit that sonofabitch. Hank and I used to go to the fights. Get ourselves a couple seats in the shitty part of the arena, way up high . . . what's that called. Something about a bloody nose . . ."

"The nosebleed section," Ben said.

"That's right. *Nosebleed*. We'd sit up there, chewing tobacco, spying all the pretty girls. Man, the two of us were a sight to behold. I'm telling you not a woman in Tupelo was safe."

The old man slowly drummed his fingers on the shotgun.

"What's wrong?" Ben said.

"Nothing."

"You seem nervous."

"Hell, no. I don't get nervous."

"What's with the shotgun?"

"I like the way it feels. You ever shoot a gun?"

"No."

The old man held up the shotgun. "Line up some cups on the bathroom sink and take a few shots."

"No thanks."

"Go ahead. I'll pay for damages."

"With what money?"

"I'll sign some fucking pillowcases. Now go on and take this."

"I said no. Don't ask me again."

The old man lowered the shotgun. "If I'd known what a pussy you are, I'd have hired someone else."

Ben smiled. "If I'd known you'd give all my money away, I'd have taken a job at the mall."

The old man snorted, a little tremor that jerked back his head. "You ever call that leggy blonde? One with the scar on her lip?"

"Alex? No."

"Too bad. She had a sexy way."

"Yes she did. I think I screwed up."

"There'll be others. Always are." He stretched his right arm overhead with a wince. Then he rubbed his eyes and sang to himself softly, his voice cracking and unsteady. *"Walk on through the wind, walk on through the rain, though your dreams be blown to shit. Walk on, ye Pharisees and motherfuckers. Walk on."* He cleared his throat. "Say, you think your little Chinese girlfriend can sew on my lion's head buckle?"

"I'll ask her," Ben said. "But she doesn't seem like the domestic type."

The old man tried to answer but decided to keep quiet; instead he hummed softly, listening to the rain.

They had to park in the farthest corner of the Little Valley Convention Center lot, a massive blacktop sheet covered in rows of cars, pickups, and choppers. Families ran, screeching children and cursing parents huddled under umbrellas and hats made from folded magazines, while the rain fell so hard Ben could hardly hear the cars splash past. They had no umbrella and no magazines, so they walked, Ginger with her arm hooked over Ben's and the old man trudging on while rain soaked his hair and new clothes, his rattlesnake silk button-down shirt, his tight white pants and shiny black boots. He wore his lion's head buckle, sewed on with dental floss by a surprisingly adept Ginger. Ben had insisted on dropping them off at the entrance but the old man refused. "We arrived as a trio and we're walking in as a trio," he said. "So if you don't mind getting wet, I'd rather we walk together."

Ben saw how nervous the old man was, how he sat in the backseat and stared out the window, fingering an orange pill bottle that Ben hadn't seen before. Whether it was from a previous stash or he'd found another dealer, it didn't matter—the old man was a serious pill fiend and, Elvis or not, Ben thought he needed to be in tip-top shape to stand any chance of winning. But it was too late because his voice was slurred and his eyes swayed like a ship in a storm. Walking through the rain, Ben figured, was a last-ditch attempt to clear his head.

Then he started to sing, this lone figure with his pale gut hanging over the mane of his gold lion's head belt buckle and rain dripping off his sagging chin. His voice lifted above the wind;

Ben realized if he sang in the contest half as good as he sounded now, not only would he win, but the entire convention center would rush the stage as if Jesus himself had returned for a one-time-only repeat performance of his Sermon on the Mount.

They stepped onto the sidewalk below a massive banner that read *Welcome Elvis Tribute Artists and Elvis Fans from Around the World!* A young man dressed in a black leather jumpsuit stood under the overhang, puffing a cigarette and tapping his foot. His hair was jet black, slicked into a spiky pompadour, an updated fifties greaser with a thorn vine tattoo encircling his wrist.

The old man made his thumb and forefinger into the shape of a gun and aimed it at the young man; he pulled the trigger. The young man winked back.

"Looking good, old-timer," the young man said, and Ben thought, If only you knew.

The old man stopped in front of the double doors and took a deep breath. Through the glass Ben saw an ocean of people. Folding tables stood in front of small stages where judges in blue polo shirts busied themselves with paperwork. Exposed metal rafters ran across the high ceiling like train tracks. The back of the room was filled with a giant center stage, and roadies worked on the lights and smoke machines, shouting and sound-checking and stomping officiously in their tan workboots. There were high-haired women and their husbands with every kind of mullet—the largest single gathering of mullets in North America, Ben figured. He saw food stands and souvenir kiosks and T-shirt air-brushing stations. Two massive screens hanging from the rafters showed dual Elvis movies—"Jailhouse Rock" and "Harum Scarum."

"I want a soft pretzel," Ginger said.

"You ready?" Ben said, and the old man put his hands on his hips and puffed out his cheeks. Then he pulled a handkerchief from his pocket and handed it to Ben.

"Gimme a dab," the old man said.

Ben dabbed his forehead.

"All right," the old man said. "Let's show them the real fucking King."

"Pissed myself."

"What?"

"I pissed myself. Felt something warm and looked down and saw *this*."

The old man pointed to the front of his pants, where Ben saw a dark splotch the shape of Florida.

"Are you sure that's not from the rain?"

"We've been waiting so long my pants are just about dry." The old man held his fingers to his nose. "And rain don't smell like piss."

They stood behind a small stage, in a curtained dressing area with folding chairs, a wardrobe rack, and a freestanding mirror. Crowd noise, bad PA systems, and canned music echoed off the metal walls.

The teenaged volunteer in her white polo and headset peeked her head through the curtain. She tapped her clipboard. "We're ready when you are, Mr. Barrow."

"Thanks, sweetie. Just gimme a minute."

"Well, okay, but we're on a reaaally tight—"

"One minute," Ginger said, and she shut the curtains.

The previous contestant walked off the stage, metal steps

clanging. He flashed Ginger a tired smile. His leis looked old and worn, curled plastic fading with age and stained with the sweat of countless confirmations, graduations, and weddings. He looked nothing like Elvis except that he was fat, with porkchop sideburns and tinted aviators, dressed in a white bejeweled jumpsuit. Ben realized he only looked like Elvis because that's what Elvis had become. Put a white bejeweled jumpsuit and tinted aviator glasses on a pig and it's Elvis Pig. Put the same on a baby and it's Elvis Baby. Put the costume on anything and the Elvis takes over.

Ben thought this explained the old man's anonymity. If he was indeed Elvis, he looked no more or less authentic than anyone else because it wasn't Elvis they worshipped. They couldn't worship what Elvis was at the end of his life—a bloated, stumbling, drug-addled stew of irrelevancy, camp, and terminal midlife crisis. So America remade him into its image, an accessible image where everyone could become their idol. Even better if he was fat. Even better if he was mediocre.

In the biographies Ben had read, everyone had something to say except for Elvis himself. The interviews with his Graceland maid, his grammar-school teachers, limo drivers, and bank tellers. Everyone had an opinion. Everyone thought Elvis had shown them something private and special. They worshipped their own worship, so it didn't matter if the King was gone, because they didn't need him anymore. Once the sneer, swivel, and heartbreaking tremolo were seared into their collective unconscious, Elvis lived forever. Flesh made plastic in diner clocks and department store Muzak. Plastic made flesh in impersonators and signed scarves sold on eBay.

Ben remembered what the old man had told him.

Pretending Elvis was alive was a hell of a lot harder than pretending he's dead.

The old man looked at the front of his pants and shook his head. "Goddamn prostate."

"Ginger, get a couple water bottles," Ben said.

"I don't think he needs any more water."

Ben dabbed the old man's brow. "Just get the water."

The old man stared across the hall, past the Aloha Hawaii Elvis section to the Sun Records Elvis section, where hopefuls swiveled and hollered. He stared as the piss cooled on his thighs and his lower back spasmed.

Ginger returned with a handful of water bottles. Ben uncapped the first and splashed it on the old man's pants. "Get the back wet," Ben said, and she poured a bottle down the back of the old man's waist.

"Goddamn, that's cold," he said.

The teenaged volunteer pushed through the backstage curtain. "Sir, we really can't wait any longer."

"We're all set," Ben said. He squeezed water from the pant cuffs and ignored the smell of urine. "There. It's like you're wearing darker pants."

The old man looked at Ginger. "Darling, be truthful with me. How do I look?"

"Hot," she said.

"Guitar," the old man said. Ben handed him the stock guitar that lay in its case under the stage risers. The old man plucked a few strings and adjusted the tuning pegs. He plucked and tuned, plucked and tuned, then rolled his head a few times and closed his eyes.

"*Sir*," the volunteer started, but the old man waved her away.

"Get that girl outta here," he said. "She's making me nervous."

Ginger put her hand on the volunteer's chest and pushed her back, through the curtain. The announcer's voice boomed hollow through the PA. "Ladies and gentlemen, next up we have John Barrow, our oldest competitor, and he'll be singing 'One Night with You.'"

Polite applause as Ben helped the old man up the stairs, his legs shaking from nerves or muscular failure or the effects of pills, Ben didn't know. All he knew was he had to get the old man on-stage and have him do his thing. He'd prop him up if he had to, hold him up by the waist and let him do the rest. Let him show everyone what Myra and Darryl had talked about, what everyone in the karaoke bar had seen and what was gone before they fully comprehended it, like an angel's face in a storm cloud, or strange lights hovering over a farmer's field in South Dakota.

And then Ben saw them. Myra and Darryl in the middle of the crowd with the rest of Hell's Foster Children. Myra's eyes lit up. Darryl cupped his hands around his mouth, shouting, "Give 'em hell!" as they began to shove their way to the front. Families were pushed aside and some of the husbands shoved back but were quickly overwhelmed by the gang of suburban bikers, who whooped and hollered and bullied past little old ladies, children, and Elvis impersonators. A throng of security guards in red polos ran from offstage, pushing into the crowd, pointing and yelling at Hell's Foster Children, who pointed and yelled back.

The old man stared off into the blurry distance. He heard a young Elvis singing "Baby Let's Play House." The requisite screams from young girls followed. He figured if he had his glasses he'd see the young Elvis jerk and grind across the stage, driving the ladies crazy with his hair flopping against his forehead like those deep-sea fish with the danglers they wiggle for little fish. Misdirection, Hank had said. Gets 'em every time.

Ben dabbed the old man's forehead again. His sweat left dark streaks like a crying lady's mascara. Ben saw the black dye under the old man's fingernails. His hair smelled of fresh chemicals.

"Ain't much of a guitar," the old man said into the microphone. He plucked and tuned once more. "Man, I like it dirty but not that dirty."

The audience quieted. Hell's Foster Children turned to the stage. The security guards in their red polos stopped where they stood and watched. Ben took one final wipe and hurried off. He stood near Ginger, who coiled an arm around his waist, resting her head on his shoulder.

"What song am I doing?" the old man asked.

"'One Night with You,'" someone shouted. There was light laughter. The old man smiled and shook his head.

Silence. Someone yelled, "'Freebird.'" Someone yelled, "Elvis, we love you!" In the background Ben heard the bustle of other stages and other crowds, but in their own bubble it was quiet as a country field before a rainstorm. Myra had willed her way to the front row. She leaned her arms on the stage, gazing upward, her long black hair thick and shiny as ever.

The old man flexed his hand with the missing pinky and strummed a chord, frowned as though surprised with himself, then cleared his throat, closed his eyes, and sang.

"I'm a poor wayfaring stranger
While traveling through this world of woe."

The crowd erupted. Myra shrieked and Hell's Foster Children roared. The judges put down their pens.

Yet there's no sickness, toil, or danger
In that bright world to which I go.

Housewives with high hair forgot how things never worked out for them, and for those few blissful moments they remembered what summer days felt like without children, bills, dirty dishes, and disappointing husbands.

I know dark clouds will hang round me
I know my way is rough and steep.

A little old lady fainted, falling at the feet of a four-year-old boy who pulled on his mother's sleeve but she was screaming. The boy pulled on his father's sleeve but his father wore the dumbfounded expression of someone who'd declared himself a god only to find the real God sitting in his living room when he returned home from work.

But I'm going there to see my mother
Where God's redeemed shall ever sleep
Yeah, where God's redeemed shall ever sleep
You motherfuckers and Pharisees.

The old man stumbled to one knee. Guitar strings popped and twanged, lashing his face as he clutched the microphone stand. It fell, squealing with feedback.
Ben and Ginger rushed to his side. The crowd surged.

"Go on and finish for me," the old man said to Ben.

Ben cradled the old man's head. A woman in the front row screamed that she couldn't breathe. Two men fell to the floor in a blur of fists. A teenage girl vomited. Hands reached for the old man's clothes and Ginger kicked them away. Myra pulled herself onto the stage, fighting past a gang of middle-aged women who clawed and scratched for a piece of the old man's rattlesnake shirt and wet white polyester pants.

The old man smiled at Ben. "Go on and finish, son. Rest of the song is just more of the same. I'll wiggle the pinky I have left and you can sing."

Ginger saw Hell's Foster Children charge the security guards. Darryl threw the first punch because that day at the construction site he'd learned the real meaning of badass watching T-Rex squirm and cough on the dirt while the old man had stood in his karate stance with sunlight glinting off his green aviators. The old man showed him what a proper leader could do. *They didn't call him the King for nothing,* Darryl had told Myra later that night, lying in bed after their evening at Lil' Rascals. *That was the first fight we almost won. You know, I'm thinking we should change our name to Hell's Righteous Children.*

The crowd heaved. Children screamed. The announcer shouted for people to remain calm while a red wave of security guards ran from the other end of the convention center. The teen-aged volunteer ran onto the stage and clutched her clipboard to her chest. "Should I call for an ambulance?" she said, but she was focused on the surging crowd and she backed away as someone threw a chair. Ben yelled at Ginger to get the car. The stage risers shook. Cups pelted the stage, spraying ice and soda. A mass of hands grabbed the guitar and Ben watched it ripped apart, punches and kicks thrown over a square of split wood, a guitar string, a plastic tuning peg.

Myra knelt by the old man and squeezed his hand.

"Heartbreaker still breaking hearts," the old man said. "You like my show?"

She leaned over and kissed him. "Best ever."

"Can you walk?" Ben asked.

The old man sniffed. "Course I can walk. I'm not a fucking cripple."

Ben and Myra hauled the old man to his feet. They stumbled down the metal stairs. On the last step the old man bent over with his hands on his knees.

"My back," he said. "It's seizing up. Can't feel my legs."

A flat *boom* echoed through the arena as the front of the stage collapsed. Ben pulled the old man away, pushing through the crowd. Cotton candy, soft pretzels, and glossy programs spilled over the beer- and soda-slicked floor. Ben lost the old man's grip and he looked back to see him struggling against a sixty-something woman with overprocessed blond hair and tight gold lamé pants. She pulled the old man close and clawed at his shirt. Her taloned fake nails dug into his chest; suddenly Myra was on her like a panther.

Ben hooked an arm under the old man's arm. They burst through the double front doors. Ginger waited for them, two tires on the curb, engine revving. The old man fell into the backseat. Ben locked his door and a strong hand gripped his shoulder. He spun with fist raised.

The young man dressed in a black leather jumpsuit held up a gold lion's head belt buckle. A thorn vine tattoo encircled his wrist. His slick-backed hair was stiff with dried gel.

"You dropped this," he said.

Ben took the buckle and the young man stuck his head into the car.

"Sir, you were amazing," he said. "Really amazing. Are you—"

"We got a scarf for this young man?" the old man said.

Ben shook his head. "We have to leave. *Now.*"

The old man ripped off his sleeve and handed it to the young man, who backed away, staring at it. Ginger floored the gas, tires smoking on the wet blacktop. The old man turned and watched out the back window, at the receding convention center sign that read *Welcome Elvis Fans—Here's Your Chance to Meet All the Elvis You Ever Wanted and More.*

13.

*B*en drove them into Mississippi toward Shake, past shotgun shacks and wire grass fields, stopping once at a gas station where weeds poked through the cracked blacktop like the hair of an underground beast. Clouds parted for them, opening to the south in a buttery trench with dark mountains on either side, but where they drove sun flashed gold across meadows and birds darted like volleys of arrows.

Ginger sat in the back of the Caddy with the old man and confessed she'd never wanted to sell her body but it was all she had and it was all the world seemed to want. She felt dirty. She felt *corrupted*, like a piece of rotten meat that spoiled whatever it touched. All those blow jobs and backseat quickies, the numbing taste of latex and spermicide, the snap of rubbers, the musk of strangers whispering atrocities in her ear. She couldn't forget it and the memories never strayed far; no matter how hard she tried to be normal, she wanted nothing more than to run away. She couldn't guarantee the old man she would stay past tomorrow. The next rest stop, the next motel, the next adventure—she might simply walk on and keep walking. Maybe she'd thumb a ride to Miami and sell necklaces on the boardwalk or make her way to Los Angeles and get a modeling gig. Maybe even sell her life story. Get cast on a reality show.

Ben listened but said nothing. He never wanted to return to Buffalo. Fucking Buffalo. The mistake on the lake, the battered old city, ruined and rusted with sterile outposts of suburban banality and pockets of urban fortresses propped up by a few streets and self-important art mags. He never wanted to return and he wanted things to stay just as they were: a Caddy, the road, the old man, and Ginger. They'd make money selling Elvis scarves and winning karaoke contests. Maybe if the old man kept his sanity long enough, they'd return to Memphis and Ben would help the old man up Graceland's hallowed steps. He'd boot all the impersonators like Odysseus slaying his wife's suitors and reclaim his place as King. Sell their story for ten million dollars like Alex had said. Exclusive interview on *Oprah*. Maybe he could write a book and call it *Tuesdays with Elvis,* turning his sadness and the old man's dementia into pre-digested mouthfuls of Sage Advice. Closure Is Bullshit. Life Goes On and That's Good Enough. Sobbing Won't Make a Seventeen-Year-Old Girl Take You Back.

Ginger finished, then broke down into tears, resting her head on the old man's shoulder. His rattlesnake shirt was ripped down the front. His sleeve dangled. The lenses of his new aviator sunglasses were already smeared. He patted her back and shushed her.

"S'all right," he said. "Everything's all right."

An hour earlier Ben had seen him chewing pills the color of robin's eggs. Ginger wiped her eyes and Ben watched her snake her hand into the old man's pocket and she pulled out his pill bottle. She uncapped it and spilled a handful of blue into her tiny palm. She looked up at him and sniffled.

The old man patted her back. "S'all right."

At a gas station with a heavy man in oil-stained overalls working the pumps, Ben bought a pack of Nutter Butters and two Gatorades, orange for the old man and red for Ginger. She drank her Gatorade as she slowly kicked across the dust and gravel, clouds swirling around her feet. She pushed through the restroom door. Forests stood on either side of the road, thick with buzzing underbrush. A rusted car husk sat slumped by the gas station garage.

The old man sat in the backseat. He rested his arm outside the window. "You got that two hundred?" he asked Ben.

Ben leaned against the door and pulled out the fold of twenties. The old man took it, stuffed it into an envelope he'd taken from his bag, then licked the envelope shut and handed it back.

"Give this to our attendant. Tell him to give it to Ginger."

"What for?"

"Whatever she needs. Girl that pretty can make her way on those eyes alone."

Ben laughed.

"No time for joking," the old man said. "Give it to him and let's ramble."

"We're not leaving her," Ben said.

The old man sighed. "I'm not bringing her anywhere near Hank. No telling what he'll do. And besides . . . she's a junkie."

Ben laughed again. "And you're not?"

"Only drugs I take are for the pain. Three compressed discs in my back."

"Bullshit. You've been stoned this entire trip."

The old man reached outside the window and slapped the Caddy's door. "Man, I'm only going to ask you once. Leave that money for her and get in the goddamn—"

"You gave her that talk about molecules," Ben said. "And all she had to do was take your hand."

"Different times."

"Not that different."

The old man fixed Ben with a stare. "Give her the goddamn money."

"No."

"Then I'll do it myself."

"You're not doing anything." Ben walked away. The old man called out for him. The restroom door opened and Ginger stretched her skinny arms overhead, ambling into the sun. The old man called out again.

"Hey," Ginger said. She held out her arms for Ben, smiling.

His cell chirped and he glanced down.

"Who's that?" she asked.

"Jessica."

She smiled slowly. "Are you going to answer?"

"No."

"Why not?"

"I don't feel like talking to Jessica right now. I feel like talking to you."

"You can't just let it ring. It's rude."

"Do you want me to talk to Jessica?"

She paused. "Not really. But you can't just let it ring—"

Ben opened the phone and turned away. "Hey, Jess."

"Ben? Did you get my message?"

"Which one?"

"The one I left last night."

"What day was that?"

"Friday, Ben. Today is Saturday."

Ben saw Ginger walking toward the car. The old man had gotten out and leaned against the door.

"I'm coming home next week," Jessica continued. "I was thinking maybe we could have dinner or something. Remember that place we used to always go . . . what was it called? The Italian restaurant with those good-looking—"

"Rigoletto's."

"That's right. So—"

"Hold on. I'm getting another call." Ben clicked over. "Hello?"

"Hey. It's Patrick. Was she serious?"

"Who?"

"Ginger. About the whole pimp thing."

"What? No. Listen, this isn't—"

"She sounded serious."

Ben watched as the old man smoothed Ginger's hair off her forehead. "She's not serious," Ben said. "I really can't talk right now. I'll call you—"

"I'm throwing a party in a few days. Think you'll be home?"

Another click. Ben put his hand to his forehead. "I guess. I don't know. I have to go." He clicked over. "Jess?"

She sighed. "It's been so awkward between us."

"I agree. Can we—"

"We used to just talk. Remember?"

"Yes. It was nice. Listen—"

"Nice?"

"Well, fuck, Jess. What do you want me to say?"

"I don't know. You always want to have these serious talks, so I just thought—"

"This isn't a good time."

"But—"

Ben hung up and ran over to the car. The old man took off his aviators and rubbed his small, tired eyes.

Ginger held out her hand. "Give me the envelope."

"I want you to stay with us," Ben said.

She shook her head.

"I'm serious," Ben said. "I heard what you told the old man about feeling like you spoil everything, and I don't care. I was thinking we could find a small town somewhere and I could get a job and save up enough money for us to go to Amsterdam—"

Ginger laughed. The old man cracked open his orange Gatorade and limped around to the passenger seat, singing softly.

"This may be the last time we stay together . . ."

"Just give me the envelope," Ginger said.

"Come with us," Ben said.

"May be the last time, I don't know."

She looked away. "The old man is right. What the hell am I doing? You're still into Jessica—he knows it. I do, too."

"Jessica has nothing to do with this. She's not here. You are, and I'm asking you to stay."

"I'm going home to meet my mother . . ."

"Why do you want me to stay?" Ginger asked.

"Because I like you."

"Do you love me?"

Ben said nothing. She pushed past him. The heavy man working the pumps stared and took out a red handkerchief, wiping the sweat from his creased forehead.

"*May be the last time, I don't know.*"

"I'm going to wait here, in front of the mini-mart," she said. "The universe will send someone my way. Someone *nice*. We'll drive to the desert and eat peyote, like that Carlos Castanet guy Elvis told me about. Do you know what else he told me?" She whirled, facing Ben. "He said there's people put on this earth to rescue others from their pain, but those people can never truly love the ones they rescue."

Ben touched her arm. "That doesn't make any sense."

"Yes, it does. Elvis said loving someone means you rescue each other. That's why you don't love me. You rescued me from Clarence. I didn't rescue you from anyone."

"I don't love you because we've only known each other for two days. But give it time."

She looked up at him, eyes wide. "Well, I love you."

Ben knew last year he would've told Ginger he loved her, too, and convinced himself it was true until he saw spinach between her teeth or she stunk up the bathroom. But at least he would've had *something*. He used to prefer half-truths to whole truths. What happened? he wondered. When did I become such a pragmatist?

He heard the old man still singing, sitting in the passenger seat, sipping orange Gatorade, belting out some dirge about going home to see his momma. It should've been sad, Ben thought, but it wasn't. Not with the hot dust and sun, and his stoned hooker, half-Thai sort-of-girlfriend throwing a fit at a gas station on the Mississippi border.

"You still love Jessica," Ginger said. "Elvis told me you do."

Ben covered his eyes for a moment, then let his fingers drag down his cheeks. "He's wrong. He's been wrong about everything. Half the time he's either stoned or living in a fantasy world. You hear him singing now? Providing our sound track? Who the hell does that?"

"He does. He's Elvis."

Ben's cell chirped. "He's *not* Elvis. He's an old man with dementia. You heard the doctor."

His cell chirped again. Ginger glanced down at it.

"I can't stand it when a phone rings and no one answers," she said. "It makes me nervous."

Ben whipped his cell as far as he could, a dark square flying across the gas station parking lot. "There. Still nervous?"

She shook her head.

"Good. Now come back to the car, and let's see if you still love me once you sober up."

A pause, a pout, then she cocked her fist back and punched Ben in the eye.

Ben held a can of soda to his swollen eye and drove with one hand. He'd spent the last half hour looking for his phone, finally finding it behind a vine-strewn tire in the fields bordering the gas station. Ginger was gone; she'd just left, hitching a ride with whomever to wherever. Fuck the nostalgia, Ben thought. My eye is throbbing.

The old man leaned his head against the window. He knew they were close to Shake. He could see it: wild trees like a witch's hair in a windstorm, shotgun shacks choked with kudzu, abandoned towns and crumbled foundations hidden in forest shadow; land fit for a monster, he thought. What we're seeing is the real Hank Rickey. What the world would've been if we'd switched places. I'm not saying I was perfect, but I brought hope as best I could. Never once claimed to be something I wasn't. Old photos summon their regrets, but who doesn't have regrets. My time stretches so far back I'm afraid I'll lose my way if I remember, so every morning I'm a baby with eyes old as the ocean.

But I remember Nadine, the old man thought. And I remember my promise. And I just might have to kill Hank before the day is through.

Ben had expected something more but Hank's house was modest—a white Greek Revival set atop a gentle hill with a single willow. Graceful green curves lay in the distance. Grass and wildflowers framed a long driveway with tire-polished gravel. Late-day gnats looped in patches of sun. Ben parked near the mailbox and popped the trunk.

The blue sky turned salmon as the old man stood behind the Caddy, hands on his hips. He and Ben stared into the trunk.

"I'm thinking twelve-gauge," the old man said.

"You stand at the front door with a shotgun and they'll call the cops."

"How about a pistol, then? Something I can hide away. Keep it close until I need it."

"How about that one?"

"The nine-millimeter?"

"Uh, yeah."

"Good choice. Reliable. Enough man-stopping power should it come to that."

"You'll need to change your shirt. The ripped sleeve makes you look crazy."

The old man frowned. "Man, I like the rattlesnake. It's like that old American flag. Don't tread on me."

They stood on the front porch. A warm breeze ruffled the old man's hair. He smoothed it back and hiked up his pants, a flash of the 9mm stuck into the elastic waistband, pressed into the soft white flab of his stomach.

"You ready?" Ben said.

The old man held up his finger. He opened his manila folder once more and straightened the papers. Their map. The *Daily Dish* article. Old photos and letters. A small, thin leather Bible with worn, curled corners. He smoothed back his hair again. "All right."

Ben used the brass knocker, a ring through a lion's mouth.

"Now, you remember the plan," the old man said.

"Plan?"

"The *plan*."

"This is the first I'm hearing of it."

The old man cupped his forehead in his hand. "Goddammit."

Ben heard footsteps behind the door.

"Anything goes sour, grab Nadine and make for the car," the old man whispered. "Get to that Days Inn on Route 74, and register under John Barrow. Give me twelve hours. I don't show, take her back—"

The dead bolt clicked and the door creaked open.

A Russian woman stood in the doorway. Late thirties, Ben guessed, with a lit cigarette dangling between her fingers. Her blond hair was pulled back tight and tied with a black bow. Smoker's wrinkles spread from her lips. She had wide-set blue eyes, and she was barefoot, wearing a red housedress. She took a puff and raised her eyebrows.

"Ma'am," the old man said. "I'm here to see Mr. Hank Rickey."

"Mr. Rickey is asleep. He is expecting you?"

"He'll know my name."

"What is your name?"

"Elvis, ma'am. Elvis Presley."

"Who is this boy with you?"

"Ben Fish," Ben said. "I'm his driver."

The woman took another puff, staring at the two of them. The old man looked down at his ripped shirt. He smiled sheepishly. "Fell down some stairs," he said. "My back isn't what it used to be."

"Okay." She dropped the cigarette and ground it out on the porch with her bare foot.

She led them through a small living room with dark wooden furniture and heavy drapes. Photos were everywhere—portraits of families standing in front of giant Christmas trees, children with Easter bunnies, handsome couples on the decks of cruise ships; they all looked alike, that wealthy-family vibe that Ben couldn't describe but knew it when he saw it. The complete opposite of Ben's family photos; small, nervous people visibly uncomfortable standing so close to one another.

The house was quiet, just the sound of their feet padding across the floor. The Russian woman walked upstairs and they followed, the old man with his hand resting on his waist under his shirt. Ben saw sweat drip down his temples and bead off his jaw.

"Where's Nadine?" the old man said. "She out getting groceries or something?"

"Nadine, the little bitch." The Russian woman stopped at the beginning of a hallway papered in floral prints. "Nadine only cares about money. But Hank's family knows this, so they send her away. Are you her family?"

"I'm her grandfather."

"Okay. So I am sorry for calling her a bitch. But she was never nice to me. Never once. I clean up Mr. Rickey's shit. I clip his fingernails. What does Nadine do? Sits on porch and talks to friends. Eats food I make, watches television. Three months she stays here, until I call Mr. Rickey's family. They come, they fight with her." She wiped her hands together. "*Pfft,* she is gone. Back to Memphis."

"Where's Hank?" the old man said.

"In his room. He is sleeping, but if you want—"

"I want." He turned to Ben. "Son, wait for me downstairs."

Ben sat in the kitchen with the Russian woman. A single window looked over the sloping yard, the outline of the willow darkening in the sunset. The kitchen was spotless, clean white walls and the plank floor waxed to a shine. Photos covered the fridge, the same faces Ben had seen throughout the house. It looked to Ben like the kind of kitchen where iced tea was always brewing, with jade-green mint leaves floating among perfect ice cubes.

The Russian woman told Ben her name was Alina, and she was from St. Petersburg. She'd been Mr. Rickey's maid and cook for ten years; before that she'd been his sometimes-lover, a young twenty-something working as a secretary in a youth ministry office that Mr. Rickey lent his singing services to. Four months ago she'd found him on the living-room floor, whispering that his face was numb and his left leg wouldn't work. He'd been with Nadine two months when he had his first stroke. They'd met in Memphis at a club that Mr. Rickey liked to frequent. Alina said that even at eighty-three years old he still liked to watch the girls dance. Nadine became his favorite girl, giving him lap dances without touching his lap because his bones were brittle.

Alina poured hot water into a pitcher and dropped in several tea bags. "Even with stroke he still liked to watch Nadine dance. Before second stroke last month I tell Mr. Rickey Nadine only does this for money. I tell him I can do the same for free. My body is not so old. What do you think?"

Ben paused, unsure of what to say.

"I was a dancer," she continued. She went up on her toes effortlessly, arms held low and graceful. Ben could see the hard edges of her calves peeking out from the hem of her red dress.

"A real dancer," she said. "Vaganova Theater in St. Petersburg, five nights a week. Not sleaze dancer like Nadine. You want iced tea?"

"Please."

"So." Alina leaned against the kitchen counter and folded her slender arms across her chest. "What is your story, Ben Fish? Are you high-school student?"

"College."

"Sorry. I am not so good with ages. What do you study?"

"Anthropology. I just graduated."

"I do not know anthropology."

"It's the study of human cultures."

"And that is your job now?"

"There aren't any jobs in anthropology. I could find some tribe and live with them, but I don't know of any that haven't already been picked over."

"So what is your job?"

"Right now I'm that old man's driver."

"Yes. The old man. He looks like Elvis, but not as handsome. Is he, you know . . ." Alina pointed to her head, twirled her finger and crossed her eyes.

"I'm still trying to figure that out," Ben said.

"So how much is he paying you?"

"Ten thousand. But I'm not getting it. It's all gone."

"That is terrible."

"It is terrible. I was planning to use that money for an apartment in Amsterdam. Have you ever been?"

She nodded. "I danced at the Het Muziektheater. Seven nights. Baryshnikov was in the audience for one show, and after he gives me single white flower. He is a short man. Onstage he looks like giant, but in person he is tall as you."

"You think I'm short?"

Alina shrugged. "Well, you are not tall."

Hank Rickey sat in a leather chair near the window with the drapes tied back. His room was large compared to the rest of the house—enough space for a king-size bed, and a walk-in closet that held his singing outfits: multicolored capes, bell-bottom white pants with garnets running down the seams, glittering silver and turquoise beads sewn in the shape of eagles, coati, and jaguars.

The old man stood in the doorway. He kept his hand on the butt of his pistol as he walked into Hank's room. Scents of menthol and baby powder. An early-evening breeze blew in through the open window, rippling Hank's brown bathrobe.

"Hank," the old man said, and Hank looked up slowly, unsteadily, his eyes clouded and his lower lip trembling.

"Hank, I've come for Nadine."

Hank smiled, his toothless mouth rimmed with jiggling flesh. His hands opened and closed, fresh-cut nails gliding over the fabric of his brown bathrobe. His features were lost in the slack and droop of age and multiple strokes. Wisps of white hair floated atop his head. Spittle collected in the corners of his lips.

"That Russian maid told me Nadine's back in Memphis," the old man said. "But you and I know the truth."

Hank blinked.

The old man pulled out the pistol and clicked back the hammer, hand trembling. He lowered it at Hank. "Tell me where she is, goddammit. And don't say nothing about Memphis. No way I'm going back there, so don't even try."

Hank turned to the window, slowly, inexorably, like the movement of a glacier. His shoulders dropped and he closed his eyes.

"Hank.

"*Hank.*"

Hank's chest rose and fell. His left hand twitched.

"Nadine Emma Brown," the old man said. His voice cracked and he blinked to clear his eyes. "I know she's here. I'll tear this goddamn house apart."

Hank began to snore, a sputtering wheeze as quiet as the wind that ruffled the drapes and the edges of his robe. The old man stumbled forward, knocked his foot on the bed and fell to his knees, gun clattering from his sweating hand, spinning on the plank floor. He scrambled for it and clutched the edge of Hank's chair.

"Now, you listen to me," the old man said. "Sitting there like you think you're something better. Never had the pussy I had. Never had the screams so loud you'd think a thousand jets took off at the same time. Made my ears ring after every show; doctors said it was hypertension but I know it was worship. Screaming my name like I'm a Greek god come down to fuck each and every one of them."

Hank's breathing slowed.

"They screamed, 'Fuck me, Elvis,' and I fucked as hard as I could. Would've made you proud to see the women I fucked. Like visions come out of the ocean on a bed of pearls, tucked in one of them giant seashells. What's the word? Sirens, is it? Or mermaids. I don't know. Something wet and hot with seaweed covering their nipples so they get past the censors. You remember the censors, Hank. Remember that night I came to you crying after that motherfucker made me sing to a dog? Remember that? Remember what you told me? Come on now. Let me hear you say it."

Hank's head dropped, chin resting on his sunken chest.

The old man wiped his eyes with the hand he held the gun in. "You said to be great is to be misunderstood."

Hank snored.

The old man sat on the floor with his legs out in front of him, head leaning against the side of the chair. The breeze cooled the back of his neck. Downstairs he heard Ben laughing. He looked into the gun barrel and let a lazy smile curl his lip.

"Look at us," he said. "We slept through the end of the world."

"Yes, I see it is beginning to bruise."

Ben touched his eye. "Like a good bruise?"

"What do you mean, good bruise?" Alina sat at the kitchen table, sipping iced tea, cigarette scissored between index and middle finger. Late dusk fell outside the kitchen window, a blue-black horizon and the last flash of a cloud's edge above the willow, slowly closing in on the dark.

"I mean does it look like someone punched me?"

"Someone did punch you. In both eyes. You look like racoon."

Ben drummed his fingers on the table. "I should have told Ginger I loved her. A little white lie wouldn't have hurt anyone."

Alina rested her chin in her hand and stared at Ben with her wide blue eyes. "Young women always talk about love. *Do you love me? I love you. He does not love me. I do not love him.* Love, love, love. Why? We do not need love to fuck. Or to have good times. If I only go with men who I love, my list is very short. Worry about love later, when excitement is gone. Then love is everything. Before that? *Pfft.* Love is a pest."

"I don't think I liked her anyway," Ben said. "I practically bought her—no, not practically. I did buy her. I paid a pimp five thousand dollars. It was the tattoo, you know. I fell for it. She has these Chinese characters across her lower back, and she doesn't even know what they mean. . . ."

Alina puffed contentedly.

"All I'm saying is I couldn't pull it off," Ben continued. "I can't date a hooker. I'm not a hooker-dating guy. Can you imagine what my mom would do? She's been through enough, and I've been useless. I'm not nearly as brave as I thought I was. I don't know where I'm going. I don't even care that I don't know where I'm going. I just graduated with a degree that will make me the smartest guy working at Burger King, I feel like I'm still in high school, and all I want to do is go back in time and call my dad and ask him just what the fuck I'm supposed to do with my life—"

Ben cupped his face in his hands. He clenched his teeth but the tears started anyway. He tightened his stomach and dug his fingers into his scalp, but they didn't stop.

Oh, please not here, he thought. Not in front of this hot Russian woman.

"I'm sorry." Ben forced a laugh and felt his palms wet. Colors blossomed in the dark of his shut eyes. Alina's hand touched his back.

"You can call your dad from here," she said. "Do not worry about long-distance charges."

Ben rested his head on the kitchen table. Alina rubbed his back and hummed.

Hank slept in his chair, summer breeze stroking his face and shadows coiling around his thin leg. The old man sat on the floor, eyes half-lidded, wrinkled hands flat on the worn planks, watching an ant move from finger to finger. The old man wished he had a crumb for the little fella. He marveled at its unwavering faith, its tireless quest for something sweet to feed its little ants back home, and soon the old man found himself tearing up. He'd felt lonely most of his life, as if only he understood the true meaning of ambition above everything else, and yet here was his companion all along: an ant. Trillions of the little bastards just like him. Amazing, he thought. Lord, thank you for sending this ant to me.

Hank snored.

"I couldn't see them even if I wanted to," the old man said to Hank. "How would they deal with a shock like that? Hey, little Lisa, it's your daddy. I been gone a long time and you stood over my grave and said sweet things, but now I got to tell you you were only talking to dirt."

But there's still time, the old man imagined Hank would say. *There's always time until there isn't.*

"I ran out of time thirty years ago," the old man said. "World sat on a hill and watched me burn, and nobody did a goddamn thing except warm themselves by the fire."

Nobody in the history of man had as much as you.

"I know. But I never asked for any of it. I didn't want it anymore."

Wasn't your decision.

"I didn't know who I was. Only saw myself through everyone else."

Last chance, then. To make it right.

"I know."

To do what's got to be done.

"All right already." The old man stood, slowly, painfully, easing around the protests in his back and warning shots firing down his leg. The gun felt heavy in his waistband, cold metal against his skin reminding him of that dark day in '86. He got lucky that day, or unlucky, depending on how you looked at it. He'd awakened in a pool of his own blood, bullet stuck into the wall over his couch.

The old man pushed his hair back and fingered the scar on his temple. He looked at Hank.

"What do you say?" He drummed his fingers on the butt end of the pistol. "Do we end it here, or do I get one last chance?"

Hank opened his eyes. His voice was wind from a cave. *Nothing for us to fight over except table scraps and memories.*

"Then can I have one of your jumpsuits?"

Take them all, the old man imagined Hank answered. *Don't you know I always loved you?*

14.

*B*itter dreams. Fire and ruin. What do you do when your enemies have shriveled and curled like old leaves at the bottom of a hedge? When the whispers stop, the sheets are yanked off the chair and you realize there's no monster beneath the dusty folds?

The old man didn't know and so he slept, refusing to wake himself from his nightmares. Instead he let them pass over, angels of death with black beating wings and open beaks that stretched back to the beginning of it all. When wriggling things wriggled in the muck and lightning shut the eyes of leviathans. When he drove a truck, bought his first guitar, and ate sandwiches of bread and salt.

Ben drove. Yellow bars pulled themselves under the car, the hum of the tires vibrating the edges of his teeth. He was beyond exhausted, beyond complaint. Just get to Memphis, he thought. Ditch this world and get back to what's real. This old man isn't real. Ginger wasn't real. Alina wasn't real. You know what's real. You remember the papasan in your apartment. Patrick being an asshole, Samantha's short hair; those are the things that fit.

Ben remembered his first anthro class, second semester freshman year. Professor Mitchell showed them a film on the Yanomamo, "The Fierce People." Yanomamo men wore a string tied around their waists and the women wore nothing. They all had saggy tits shaped like gourds, every one of them. It never made sense, Ben thought. How come naked women in the jungle never have good bodies? It's always flat asses, gourd-shaped breasts, and little potbellies.

Ben rubbed his eyes and slapped his face while the road dipped and curved. The old man mumbled in his sleep.

Professor Mitchell had told them that more than a third of Yanomamo males die from violence. Then they watched old footage of a Yanomamo war, a raid against a neighboring village. Professor Mitchell warned them it was about to get bloody and a few of the girls turned away. He sat and watched as the warriors hacked away with machete blades lashed to the end of long reeds. It looked like a mosh pit where everyone was naked.

All it would take is Elvis, Ben thought. Pull a 9mm and make sure it didn't get bloody. Sing for the tribal elders and they'd make him honorary shaman. Shoot yopo up his nose and go on one of those vision quests where you find your spirit animal. Then continue the world tour; next stop, Kung San, the Bushmen of the Kalahari. How do you say Elvis in click?

Suddenly weeds clawed at the underside of their Caddy and the hood dipped. Metal squealed. Ben's seat belt ripped into his shoulder. The car stopped and his head slammed against the driver's-side window.

He smelled antifreeze; the engine ticked. The old man turned to him and there was blood streaming down his face, blood dotting the new white jumpsuit he'd taken from Hank's. Red and green garnets were sewn into the back in the shape of an Aztec thunderbird, its plumage running down the side of the leg. The old man's lion's head buckle shone dull in the moonlight.

"Are we dead?" the old man asked.

Ben stared out the windshield. Steam rose from the engine, soft yellow from the headlights shining against the grass. "I don't think so."

"How do you know?"

"Because my shoulder hurts." Ben unlatched the seat belt and opened the door. Its edge dug into the soft dirt, tearing up a clump of weeds. They were in a ditch, the forest ahead and the road behind. Ben heard crickets. He looked to the distance, blue hills bathed in moonlight like the backs of giant whales sleeping in the ocean.

The old man shoved his door open and stumbled out.

"Hey," Ben said. "You shouldn't be walking around."

The old man made his way to the front of the Caddy. He pinched his bleeding nose and shook his head. "Goddammit. God-fucking-*dammit*."

"I'll get us a tow. Let me just make a few calls."

"Man, you said you had a clean driving record."

"I just nodded off. We've been going pretty hard and—"

The old man spit a ropy string of blood. "Boy, you don't know the meaning of going hard. Fifteen cities in ten days. That's going hard. Press conference at seven, karate at nine, cut an album from midnight until the sun shows its tits. That's going hard."

"Shut up," Ben said. "For once, just shut up, and let me think this through."

The old man took his hand off his nose. "What's that?"

"I'm sick of your stories. The touring, the anguish . . . it's all bullshit."

"Bullshit?"

"You don't even look like Elvis. The real Elvis wouldn't throw it all away. For what? A life in the burbs? Because you were burned out? Give me a break. My dad got pinned to a fucking hot dog stand by some woman gabbing on her cell phone. You don't see me whining. Well, maybe a little. But not all the time. Not like you."

"Hot dog stand. You never told me that."

"You never asked."

"What'd they do to that woman?"

"Nothing."

"You know where she is now?"

Ben shrugged.

"You find out and I'll make some calls. I still got connections in dark places."

Ben laughed.

"Man, I'm serious."

"Of course you are. That'll be our next mission. Revenge against the woman who killed my dad." Ben looked to the sky and shook his head. "What the hell are we doing?"

"We're going for Nadine."

"You're going for Nadine. I'm done."

"Can't be done. Not until I say. That's how it works. That's how it's always worked. Rest of the world quits when it gets rough—not me, and not you."

"I should be selling ties. Instead I'm standing in a ditch in the middle of Tennessee, and I don't even know who you really are."

"Nobody did." The old man spit blood again. "Nobody bothered asking."

Ben started to speak but stopped himself. It was all useless, he realized. They could talk forever in that ditch until the worms ate their bones. He marched up the side of the ditch and started to walk down the shoulder.

"Hey!" the old man shouted. He clawed his way up the hill, a muscle pulsing in his side that felt like a hot spear every time he breathed. He tasted his own blood and spit it out. He knew his nose was broken. Maybe even his ribs.

"You can't leave," the old man said. "What about Nadine?"

Ben kept walking. "Fuck Nadine."

"Fuck Nadine?"

Ben stopped and turned. "You heard me. *Fuck Nadine.*"

The old man roared and charged. He threw a kick; Ben stepped back and the old man felt something give in his hamstring. All the strength went out from under him. He stumbled to one knee. The old man tried to stand but lost his balance and fell onto the side of the road. Gravel bit his cheek. He pushed himself up and lunged for Ben, but the boy was too far away and he fell again. He felt skin tear from his palms. Road dust stung his eyes.

The old man rolled onto his back, coughing. He gazed at the moon. One nostril was plugged with blood; as he breathed through the other, it made a faint whistling sound like a teakettle. "I'm coming apart," he said. "Help me up, son. Jesus Christ, I'm in sorry shape. Come on now. Help me up. Where are you going?"

Ben looked over his shoulder. "Home."

Ben walked all night, past forests and mats of kudzu, his steps marked by the crunch of gravel and cicada chants. He felt like a post-apocalyptic drifter haunting the back roads of Tennessee, only this version of a post-apocalyptic world wasn't filled with armored dune buggies and crossbows. This version was how it would really be: empty roads and overgrown forests, a few survivors among the mutants like that movie he remembered seeing when he was seven, the one with Charlton Heston, the pretty lady with the Afro, and all those pale-faced vampires with severely chapped lips.

Maybe I'm dead, Ben thought. Maybe I died in that ditch, my chest crushed against the steering wheel. Maybe this is hell and Satan is dressed like Elvis.

The night slinked past. Birds awoke and the cicadas stopped. He watched dawn begin with a light blue line creeping over the mountaintops, and he began to jog. He felt good, surprisingly good, running faster until the wind shooshed in his ears. It seemed perfectly reasonable that he could run all the way back to Cheektowaga. The forest sharpened as if coming into focus, from dark blue mounds to pale green clumps to individual leaves. Ben passed a town sign and the forest tapered into mowed grass and suddenly there were buildings ahead, brick storefronts and modest clapboard homes. A church stood proudly apart with a bench on its sidewalk, church sign stuck into the lawn. Morning light washed over everything. The air smelled like dew.

Trinity Baptist Church. Howard E. Hipp, Pastor.

Ben had never seen such a perfect bench with its curled wrought-iron armrests and pristine white wooden slats. He sat down, closed his eyes, and raised his face to the strengthening sun.

He sat there for what felt like a long time. Wind stirred. Somewhere far away a dog barked. Then he heard voices. Women. Old women talking excitedly. He opened his eyes and saw a group of them walking down the sidewalk toward him, only they didn't seem to notice him. They wore housedresses, hats, and poofy white blouses, giant purses dangling from their forearms. Some walked in sneakers, others in orthopedic shoes with thick heels. They stopped a few feet from Ben and kept talking. Ben couldn't pick up on one thread of conversation. It seemed like all they said was *Oh* and *My* and *Mmm-hmm*, laughing with one hand pressed to their chess.

One of the women looked down at Ben. She wore a white blouse buttoned all the way up, with draping sleeves like a flying squirrel. Her long baby-blue skirt matched her shoes and stockings. A plastic daisy sat tucked into the band of her white hat.

She smiled. "Are you waiting for the bus?"

"No, ma'am."

"Well, then, what are you doing?"

"Resting."

"Resting?"

"Yes, ma'am. I'm resting for my trip."

"Where are you going?"

"Cheektowaga. It's near Buffalo."

"Hmm . . . No buses leave for Buffalo from here."

"I'm walking."

"Walking? To *Buffalo*?"

"That's right. It's only nine hundred miles. Give or take."

The old lady held her hand to her chest and tugged on the sleeve of a woman standing next to her. "Florence, this young man—what did you say your name was? Ben? Florence, this young man is Ben and he says he's walking nine hundred miles to Buffalo."

Florence glanced at Ben with a frown. Her mouth was tight. She wore a red wide-brimmed hat and a red dress, the mottled skin on the back of her hands bubbled with blue veins.

"What happened to your eyes?" Florence asked.

"A biker punched me in the right, my ex-girlfriend punched me in the left."

"You probably deserved it," Florence said, and she turned back to her conversation.

The sun climbed. Their shadows shrank. The group of chattering old women fanned themselves with folded pieces of paper. In the distance Ben saw a figure lurching down the road. He knew it was the old man because the old man said he never quits. The old man would outlast them all, walking forever until his feet ground to stumps. Nadine his oasis, Nadine the salvation for all old men. He should be pushing the hot dog stand my dad got smashed against, Ben thought. He should be pushing it and shouting to me that my dad is still alive somewhere, that we can find him if we only believe.

As he moved closer, Ben could see his new jumpsuit was gray with sweat, a mat of chest hair in a dark jumble spilling out from the unzipped neck. Dust covered the red and green garnets. White gunk collected in the corners of his mouth and his eyes were half-lidded. He dragged his right leg, carrying his dossier, edges of papers sticking out from the manila folder. The old man looked like he was melting, finally devolving back to the impossible lump he'd grown from. An alchemist's creation, a homunculus forged from phoenix feathers, hair dye, and paper bags soaked with french fry grease.

The old man sat on the bench next to Ben and dropped his chin to his chest. A scabbed gash lay across the bridge of his nose. His voice sounded like he'd smoked a box of cigarettes.

"Hot goddamn morning."

"Sure is," Ben said.

"Man, I could sure use some water. Big old glass filled with crushed ice."

"Water would be nice."

"You want me to get you some?"

"With what money?"

"I'll sing one of them Native rain dances. You can hold the cup."

Ben folded his arms.

The old man closed his eyes. "Thought I'd lost you. Thought you got picked up and murdered. Left in a ditch somewhere."

"I can take care of myself."

"I know. Thing is . . ." The old man shook his head. Sweat dripped off the tip of his nose. "Thing is, I'm sorry."

"It's okay."

"It's not. You been nothing but loyal. I shouldn't have kicked you."

"You were too slow anyway."

"Lucky for you," the old man said. "I Iit you so hard your first-born come out with a birthmark on his stomach the shape of my boot. Tell him, 'Son, that's a gift from the baddest man there ever was.'"

They laughed a little. The old lady with the plastic daisy in her hat looked at the two of them. "There's a vending machine in the church," she said. "Do you need a dollar?"

Ben smiled. "Yes, ma'am."

She reached into her purse and carefully plucked a dollar from its depths. Ben walked to the church. The lobby was cool and quiet and his sneakers squeaked on the polished floor. A photo of Pastor Howard E. Hipp hung on the wall, a man in his fifties with a seersucker suit and giant glasses. Ben bought a bottle of water, holding it to his forehead as he walked back into the sun. A silver bus parked at the curb in front of the bench. The old women slowly formed a queue.

The old man licked his cracked lips. The bus engine idled. Waves of heat shimmered off the pavement.

The lady with the plastic daisy in her hat stopped on the bus steps and smiled. "Are you coming?"

"Where?" Ben said.

"Graceland," she said. "Our church group visits every year."

"Of course you do," Ben said. He passed the water bottle to the old man, who gulped it dry and wiped his mouth.

"Last charge of the righteous," the old man said. "You ready?"

You will question my judgment, Ben remembered him saying. *You will question my purpose, my morals, and my lucidity. But always remember that though these old eyes look cloudy, they've seen to the end of the universe.*

"I'm ready and I'm tired," Ben said.

The old man tossed the water bottle aside. "Then I'll carry you."

Florence sighed and gazed out the window. Ben sat near her, in the front of the bus, knees up against the seat-back in front of him.

"You're too young to be wasting your time worrying about this Ginger," Florence said. "She's no good. She's fickle, and a fickle woman will only disappoint. I know because I was a fickle woman. A *very* fickle woman. I'd date a boy for a few months and if I got bored—and I *always* got bored—I'd leave him without a care. Oh, sure they would cry and carry on, and sometimes that was enough to keep me interested so I'd at least answer their letters. But eventually I'd forget them. Eventually we all forget."

Industrial buildings spread along the highway, low and flat under a cloud-dotted sky. A cardboard-colored skyscraper sat in the distance. Power lines loped past. The old man sat somewhere in back, and Ben watched as the women made various excuses to walk past, glancing nervously, whispering to each other.

"I've lost two husbands," Florence said. "And a child, and a grandchild. Every time I think it's too hard. You know what? It *is* too hard. But we go on, don't we?"

"We do," Ben said. "Look at me. Sitting on a bus with you and Elvis, going to Graceland."

Florence turned to him. "Honey, that's why he put the grace in Graceland."

"I know it's you."

The old man opened one eye. The lady with the plastic daisy in her hat had sat near him and the old man felt her staring even as he nodded off. She'd stared for an hour, silent as a monk, while her friends talked about the pastor's wife and their three adorable kids, though one looked mixed race and they wondered if he was a foster child of some sort, rescued from God knows where.

The lady sat with her tiny hands folded in her lap. "The Lord told me one day the King would return home. Today is that day."

"You're a patient woman," the old man said.

"All good things. What happened to your hand?"

"Lost my pinky. Chopped it off with a steak knife."

"I'm sure you had your reasons. Would you like a candy?"

"What kind?"

"Sugar-free peppermint."

"You got any Tootsie Rolls?"

She shook her head.

"Man, that's too bad," the old man said. "I love them Tootsie Rolls."

15.

A massive blue sign stood behind a chain-link fence. *Graceland. Home of Elvis A. Presley.* Cars sped down the boulevard, the same boulevard where Elvis in bathrobe and slippers rode his ATV in those late nights of 1977, a bloated ghost zooming through the dark. Ben had read about it after his first coffee with the old man, that morning eons ago when he'd sat in the diner booth with the '65 wisteria-on-white Caddy waiting in the parking lot.

The old women poured out of the bus, cameras in hand, purses swinging from their forearms. Behind them stood a German couple, a short woman with chopped blond hair and her husband with dark horn-rim glasses, snapping photos of the oldest Elvis impersonator he'd ever seen. The old man stood and stared as the chattering group wandered down the driveway, lost in their conversations.

"You want to take a look?" Ben asked.

The old man shook his head.

"Aren't you even a little curious? Maybe they've changed it around."

"Nothing changed," the old man said. "Same furniture, same pictures, same silverware. I walk in there and feel how old I am. I walk in there and feel like I got the worst fucking taste in the world. Priscilla should've fucking known better than to keep things the way they were. If I lived there now, I'd have one of those future kitchens—you know, from that Swedish store."

"IKEA."

"That's right. I'd have one of those IKEA kitchens."

The lady with the plastic daisy in her hat hung back from the group. She held a camera. "May I?"

The old man grabbed Ben around the shoulders and pulled him close.

"This one's going on the mantel," the old man said.

"Lord, yes," the lady said, and she clicked.

Alina had given them the last-known address of Nadine Emma Brown. The old man and Ben walked all afternoon to a place called Orange Mount. They walked down quiet tree-lined streets, past buildings with hand-painted signs selling doughnuts and hair extensions and cell phone packages, rusted signs with their lights punched out and boarded buildings covered in graffiti. A black family stood on the corner, pointing at the old man limping along in his jumpsuit with the Aztec thunderbird on the back.

The old man held his pills and let them drop, one by one, blue and red discs bouncing on the sidewalk like that Greek myth he remembered with the maze and the minotaur. Or was it twine the hero used, or was it those two kids in the forest who find a house made of gingerbread and some old bitch tries to eat them. He could never get his myths straight, but it didn't matter because he realized myths are about two things—you get lost or you get found. Throw in some sword fights, half-naked chicks, and a few monsters, but it's always the same story. Some poor son of a bitch can't find his way; some lucky son of a bitch can.

They turned down a street with a brick-and-cement-block building on the corner. *James's Lounge Memphis's Party Spot.* Dead vines clawed up the side, a spindly bent tree stuck in the edge of the parking lot. At the end of the street stood a cedar-shingle home with a toppled grill on the front lawn and a hose lying like a dead snake, *N. Brown* printed on the mailbox. The old man stopped at the driveway. He smoothed back his hair and patted his jumpsuit. He straightened the papers in his manila folder. He took his aviators from his pocket and smoothed back his hair again.

"Give me a dab."

"I don't have anything to dab you with."

"Goddammit, give me a *dab*—"

"All right. Just relax." Ben pulled his shirtsleeve to his hand. He patted the old man's forehead.

The old man stared at the house. "Do you believe I was the King?"

"Yes."

"Come on, now. Don't lie to me. Not here."

"I'm not lying."

The old man looked at him. "Swear to God."

"On a stack of Bibles," Ben said.

"You an atheist?"

Ben smiled.

"Man, I'm serious. What happened to your daddy make any boy an atheist."

"I'm not an atheist."

The old man zipped his jumpsuit to his throat. "Never made any sense, those atheists. Think they have answers just like the religious folk. How do I look?"

"You look ready."

"Good, 'cause I think I might throw up." The old man put one hand to his stomach and limped with his chin held high, down the driveway and up the front steps. He put on his aviators and knocked on the door.

Ben watched the front door creak open. A short, thin woman stood in her bare feet, one foot resting atop the other. She wore pink nail polish and white terry-cloth shorts rolled at the top. Her black Jack Daniel's T-shirt hung to her waist. She stood with one hand on her hip. Her forehead wrinkled in confusion as Ben heard the old man talking. She crossed her arms and tossed her hair back. The old man stepped closer. She held up her hand. He dropped his manila folder.

"Sorry," Ben heard the old man say. The old man bent down and collected the papers and photos, still apologizing, and the woman looked toward the street. Ben wished he wasn't there because it made it look more suspicious than it already was. An old Elvis impersonator with his black-eyed accomplice waiting on the sidewalk. He smiled as innocently as he could.

She backed away and started to close the door, but the old man grabbed the doorjamb and she yelled at him to let go. He kept talking. She yelled again.

"Get the fuck out of here."

"Just hold on—"

"Didn't you hear me? I said, *Get the fuck out of here.*"

The old man stopped. He looked down at his dossier, at the folded maps, newspaper clippings, and notes in red marker. The pages printed off the Internet and the copies of love letters. The yellowing photos with creases spread across everyone's face.

She slammed the door shut but the old man stuck his shoe in the threshold. He raised his voice. "Nadine, this isn't a good life for you. I got something better—"

The old man started to enter the house and Ben saw her arm jut from the dark. She held something at his face and he let out a choked cry, stumbling back, his folder falling once more and scattering papers. He fell down the steps, coughing and gagging into his hands. Ben sprinted. The door slammed shut.

"*Mace,*" the old man cried. He rolled onto his stomach. Ben saw the woman watching from her front window. The old man kicked his feet against the steps. Ben grabbed the hose, cranked it on, and blasted him in the face. The old man spit, sputtered, then lay on his back with his arms spread as if he were making snow angels.

Ben looked at the woman in the window. She raised her middle finger, then shut the curtains.

The old man stayed quiet as they walked through town, past spray-painted murals commemorating Martin Luther King Jr. parks and Frederick Douglass boulevards. Ben found a crinkled dollar in his back pocket so he bought a can of Pepsi and a Doritos snack pack. The old man stopped every few blocks, resting on a stoop or on the edge of a low wall, and Ben said he needed to see a doctor but the old man shook his head and said he was done being poked and prodded. His face was swollen from the Mace. His eyes were red-rimmed, his lips bee-stung.

He stopped at a corner bus stop and collapsed onto the bench. He opened the manila folder across his lap. Ben sat near him. The sun lingered behind buildings and in the limbs of tall trees. The air smelled like heat.

"We need a plan," Ben said.

"Eddie Fulsom." The old man pulled out his wallet, thumbing through cards. "He lives a couple blocks from here. He'll help us out."

"Then what?"

"Home." He picked up a photo of a young Nadine, standing on a patchy lawn, wearing a bathing suit and squinting into the camera. Ben thought the woman he saw in the cedar-shingle home looked a little like her, but he couldn't tell because all kids in bathing suits looked the same to him.

"What did Nadine say to you?"

The old man shrugged. "Said her grandfather died when she was a little girl. She's seen pictures and I don't look like him."

"Maybe she's lying."

The old man said nothing.

"Let me talk to her."

The old man shook his head.

"Your approach was all wrong. You freaked her out. You were too intense. You were sweating like a horse—"

"Maybe 'cause I'm an old fat man and it's a hundred fucking degrees."

"Just let me talk to her. I'll play it cool."

"Cool, huh."

"Give me a chance, Elvis. You got nothing to lose."

"What'd you call me?"

"Elvis."

"Boy, I ain't Elvis."

"Yes you are."

The old man laughed bitterly. "Elvis is fucking dead. Died August 16, 1977, from heart failure. Ginger Alden found him a few feet from his toilet, pajama bottoms around his ankles, face stuck in a puddle of puke. Coroner found fourteen drugs in his system. Morphine, Demerol, and Chlorpheniramine. Placidyl. Valium. Codeine and Ethinamate and Amytal. Nembutal. Carbrital. Sinutab. Elavil, Avental, and Valmid. I remember the day I heard about it. I was driving a truck to Birmingham. Load of vacuum cleaners. Married to my second wife, Beth Anne. Met her in Raleigh at a cousin's wedding. Got a daughter with her— Shelly. Beth and I divorced in 1983. Love of my life, that woman; I think about her every day."

"You're lying."

The old man turned to him.

"My dad is an accountant," Ben said. "He doesn't have to work because his father invented a new pressure seal for oil pumps and made a fortune. But my dad believes work develops character, so he's at the office every morning at seven A.M. My mom volunteers at the local VA. She cooks for the older veterans. I've had a trust fund my whole life, and I feel guilty because all my friends have to scrape and I don't. So I tell everyone my dad died in a horrible accident. People treat you better when they find out something bad happened."

The old man sighed. "Man, you are a terrible liar."

"So are you," Ben said.

16.

*E*ddie Fulsom spit into his empty Folgers can and shook his head again. He looked to Ben like some famous blues musician, an old black guy with a cool nickname and a voice that sounded like gravel in a blender.

"I cannot believe how old you got," Eddie said to the old man, and he laughed until he launched into a coughing fit. "Look at that turkey neck. And those bags under your eyes—you need a bellhop to carry those?"

"That's not all I need a bellhop to carry." The old man put his boots up on Eddie's desk. They both laughed. The desk was covered with old magazines, invoices, and Styrofoam cups with dried coffee stains. Eddie's office was also his home, a white unhitched trailer sitting behind a car-parts store. Fulsom Car Recovery. Rusted car husks filled the lot. Stacks of tires swarmed with mosquitoes.

"I got a Gremlin available right now," Eddie said. "And a '94 Taurus with no AC."

"We need something to get us back to Buffalo," the old man said. "Something comfortable."

"Maybe if I had a week I could get you a decent ride. But on short notice the best I can do is that Taurus."

"Bullshit."

Eddie sighed, then mumbled to himself and leaned back, looking over the rack of keys mounted on the wall. "If you can wait until tomorrow morning, I can get you a '98 Continental."

"We can wait," the old man said.

Eddie nodded and scribbled something on a sheet of paper. He held the Folgers can on his stomach. "Everything work out with that girl you were looking for?"

The old man said nothing. Eddie raised his eyebrows at Ben.

"Told you." Eddie spit into his can. "Hank may be old but he's still got it. Couldn't get women off him when we were kids, and can't get them off now."

"She's not with Hank," Ben said.

"Then where is she?"

The old man sniffled. "Here."

"In Orange Mount?"

The old man nodded.

"God*damn*," Eddie said. "And I thought you came back to say hi."

"You got a bathroom?" the old man asked.

Eddie pointed to the other side of the room. The old man stood, slowly, legs shaking with effort. He righted himself and began his stiff walk across the room.

Ben stared at Eddie. Eddie stared at Ben.

"Never thought you'd be driving his fat ass around for summer break, did you?"

"Nope."

"He's like that. Always got you doing the exact opposite of what you thought."

"How long have you been friends?" Ben said.

Eddie whistled. "Too long. How long you been his driver?"

"Six days."

He laughed. "You know that son of a bitch—"

"You mean Elvis."

Eddie smiled. "I mean that son of a bitch. Anyway, that son of a bitch helped me rebuild my first dream car. Can't remember what it was, but he helped me rebuild it. Handy son of a bitch that son of a bitch. And a hell of a voice."

"He told me who he is."

"And what did he say?"

"He said he's Elvis Presley."

"What a coincidence." Eddie winked at Ben and spit into his Folgers can. "Didn't he tell you I'm Malcolm X?"

Ben and the old man sat in a bar down the street from the Shake-A-Tail Motel. Eddie had talked to Reginald, the motel owner, who gave the old man two free rooms on the top floor. Tomorrow morning at nine A.M. someone named Mayorga would drop off their car, a full tank of gas, and two hundred in cash for their trip home. "Now, I don't want anything in return," Eddie had said to the old man, and the old man said, "You're fucking with my karma," and Eddie said, "Your karma been fucked for a thousand years."

Then they hugged and Eddie looked at the old man as if it were the last time they'd see each other. When the old man turned away, Ben swore he saw tears in his eyes.

So they spent the night at the bar, drinking for free because the bartender liked the old man's jumpsuit and felt bad they'd been in a car wreck, and the old man kept eyeing the dusty piano across the room, forgotten in a dark corner like an ugly woman on singles' night. Ben drank his beer and nudged the old man but the old man shook his head, claiming his back hurt too much to play. Too goddamn much to do anything but sit and drink even though he nursed one beer and his speech began to slur like the old days. Too goddamn much to think about Nadine or Hank, or how Eddie and Ben were his only true friends in the entire world.

It rolled past midnight and the bar emptied. Soon the old man and Ben were the last customers in the room. The bartender talked with his girlfriend at the end of the bar, white towel slung over his shoulder, and Ben wished she'd look at the old man and saunter over, writing her number in red lipstick on the bar. He wished they'd all stop and stare, the entire city pouring in, fighting and screaming to get a glimpse. Front page of the *New York Times* and *Breaking News* on CNN, even the Google logo done in a clever send-up of the King. Jumpsuits and aviator glasses on every letter; the sneering *G*, mutton-chop sideburns on the *O*, drugged-out *L* lying on a pile of scarves with a guitar.

Instead there was nothing. Only the quiet clink of his beer bottle and the old man shifting on his bar stool to ease the shooting pains in his back.

"I miss her, you know," the old man said.

"Nadine?"

"My girl. My baby girl." He smiled a little, drool collecting in the corner of his mouth. He wiped it off and let his hand flop back onto the bar. "Hurts so much I could cry. *'I get so lonesome I could die.*' You know how much I hated that song? Always thought it was corny. Now I get it. The old man gets it."

He started to say something else—something about a lifetime of regrets erased with a little bit of courage—but his eyes rolled back and he slumped forward. Ben caught him before he fell.

"Hold on." Ben struggled to keep the old man on his stool. *"Hey,"* he shouted to the bartender. "We got a problem—"

"Fresh as a daisy," the old man whispered. He opened his eyes.

"How many did you take?" Ben asked.

"Not enough. My back still hurts like a motherfucker."

"Do you want me to find you some more?"

The old man smiled. "Man, that's okay. You done enough."

Then he slipped off the stool and took a deep breath, making his way across the bar, holding on to tabletops as he lumbered past, red and green garnets falling from the Aztec thunderbird emblazoned on his back. He smoothed his hair and stopped at the piano. He winced as he sat on its bench, flipped open the fallboard, made his hands into fists and opened them wide as he could. He cleared his throat, letting his fingers rest on the dusty keys, closing his eyes, remembering a laughing beauty queen in the passenger seat with the wind caressing her long brown hair and her legs dangling out the window. Pink polish on her pink little toes. Glittering anklet. Pink shorts hiked up to the top of her smooth tan thighs.

Back when I rambled, the old man thought. A rambler roaring through the world, drinking oceans dry and chopping down mountains.

Somewhere in the smoke and light.
Oh the king he sings of Heaven.

Oh yes he believes there is a paradise.
And a band is playing there.

There is a black car waiting somewhere outside.
Filled with lovely ladies for celebration.
He wipes the tears from his eyes.
For all his lonely lovemaking.
Oh babe. Whenever will you love me?

The old man closed the fallboard. Ben clapped and whistled.

The bartender leaned close to his girlfriend and whispered, "Every week some poor guy wanders in and pretends he's the King. But you know, that old man wasn't so bad."

Ben woke to the sound of a car horn. Eddie stood on the sidewalk in front of the motel, black Lincoln Continental parked in front. Ben ran down the stairs barefoot, pulling his T-shirt over his head and combing his hands through his hair. He stepped onto the sidewalk and squinted against the sun.

A Mexican sat at the wheel of an old Mercedes, idling behind the Lincoln. Eddie tossed the keys to Ben and handed him an envelope stuffed with crisp twenties.

"It was a 1958 Ford Skyliner," Eddie said. "My first dream car. The one that son of a bitch helped me rebuild. You know he gave me the engine from his own Skyliner? That's the kind of guy he is. Tear his heart out if you said yours was broken. Understand?"

Ben nodded.

"Good," Eddie said. "'Cause a lot of people didn't. Now, you tell him I said not to wait thirty years next time."

Ben shook Eddie's hand and watched as he got into the old Mercedes and drove away, into the shimmering heat.

Ben ran back upstairs and knocked on the old man's door. He waited. He knocked again and said, "Elvis?" Then he tried the knob and it clicked open. The door swung slowly with a long creak.

The bed was empty except for two garnet stones lying on the sheets, glittering in a bar of morning sun.

Ben drove until the sun dipped behind low-slung buildings and an evening wind ruffled the trees. He drove slowly, window down. Everywhere he looked he saw the old man. Posing for a picture in front of the Sun Records building; sitting on a restaurant patio eating a burger and fries; walking out of a Gap; feeding quarters into a parking meter. Hundreds of Elvii, wiping sweat from their foreheads because it was too damn hot to wear a jumpsuit, but where else could you wear such a ridiculous outfit and no one would laugh at you.

Eddie's store was closed, so Ben pulled to the back and knocked on his trailer door. He shouted Eddie's name and was answered by the surging chirps of crickets. He drove to the bar and found it empty save a few middle-aged men flicking bottle caps across the room while the bartender talked on his cell. He drove to Graceland and it was closed for the day, gated with a security car sitting at the entrance.

Ben drove to Orange Mount and parked outside Nadine's home. He summoned his courage but lost it every time, afraid she'd be waiting with a can of Mace or a giant boyfriend. The wind picked up and leaves scraped across the driveway. Ben cursed and punched the steering wheel, laying on the horn until he saw her porch light flicker. She opened the door, peeking out her head. She wore the same clothes as the day before, only her hair was wrapped in a towel. She looked at the car. Ben peeled away, laughing for no good reason, into the night.

17.

en smelled Chinese cooking oil from miles away. A line of cars were parked outside his apartment and the faint cacophony of a party got louder as he trudged up the stairs. Nineteen cents in his pocket remained from the two hundred in crisp twenties—he'd eaten well during the trip home, gorging himself on shrimp platters and steak tips and 7-Eleven hot dogs. Every rest stop he expected to find the old man pushing through the restroom door, hair freshly combed, a Big Gulp in hand. That slow drawl coated in pills, limping and complaining about the pain in his back but relentless as always. *You know, I remember one time Lamar and I carried a cow on our shoulders from Austin to Duluth. Chopped down a mountain over Labor Day weekend back in '72. Drank the Mississippi in a single night and puked it back up before sunrise, fish and all.*

There was one night at a Denny's in Frankfort, Kentucky, when Ben saw the back of a man wearing a red jumpsuit with thinning dyed hair combed into a struggling pompadour. He walked across the restaurant and saw the man was a thick-joweled loner with glasses, hunched over a Grand Slam, grasping his vanilla shake. "The fuck you looking at?" the man hissed, and Ben stared, wishing the man would make a move. But the man only wanted to eat and drink his shake in peace, and Ben felt foolish for flexing the courage that had failed him outside that cedar-shingle home in Orange Mount.

He opened his apartment door to noise and music. Patrick stood in the middle of the living room. Samantha sat on the threadbare plaid couch, legs folded under her skirt. Steve and Jim huddled near the three-legged Naugahyde chair, sharing a joint, Jim wearing his favorite basketball shirt with the jacked guy dunking on a hundred-foot rim. The aquarium was still green with algae.

"Holy fucking *shit*," Patrick said.

The room fell silent. Ben pushed past them all and headed for his bedroom. He heard Patrick call out to him, and Samantha say *Benjamin* and then something about his mom having called but he'd driven for two days without sleep. The dark of his room and the cool pillowcase were the two things he wanted more than anything in the world.

He awoke to the sound of traffic outside his window. He stumbled from bed and walked through the living room. Empty cups and a bong sat on the kitchen table, surrounded by crumbs and plastic bowls with melted ice cream. Afternoon sun warmed the counter. The microwave read two P.M. He'd slept for fifteen hours. He took a carton of orange juice from the fridge, rinsing his mouth, then grabbed a bag of pretzels and walked back to the living room.

A small box sat near the door. The FedEx label showed *John Barrow* as the sender.

The buzzer sounded. Ben buzzed and opened the door. He sat on the couch with the box and ripped it open, rummaging through crinkled balls of newspaper. One of the back-page headlines—from the *Memphis Sun*—was highlighted in yellow marker: *Car Found in Mississippi with Arsenal in Trunk.*

"Ben?"

She stood in the doorway, wearing white Keds and an electric-blue T-shirt. Her blond hair was shorter than he remembered. She was prettier than he remembered; her cheeks flushed, like they always did when she got nervous. It all came back. He thought it was funny how he'd forgotten the little things. He'd always believed you remembered the little things and forgot the rest.

"Hey, Jess."

"Hey. I've been trying to reach you."

"My cell died."

"I figured it was something like that. I got back a few days ago." She smiled. "I see you still haven't cleaned that aquarium. Do you like my hair?"

"Love it."

She pushed a strand behind her ear. "So, do you want to get some lunch?"

"How's Alan?"

"I don't care. It's a long story, and if I never have to talk about him again . . ."

"That's cool."

Silence, then Jessica clapped her hands together. "So, lunch?"

"I can't."

"Oh." She toed the carpet. "I just thought you might be hungry. We can walk around the mall instead, or do whatever."

"I am hungry," Ben said. "But I can't have lunch. You do look great, though. That Alan is missing out."

Jessica frowned. "I told you I don't care about Alan. Why are you acting so weird?"

Ben stood and walked up to her. He could smell the cocoa butter scent that always made his mouth water. The raspberry lip gloss was gone, however. She was older now, a college girl with unscented lip gloss. She was more than pretty—she was beautiful. He could pretend and play the cool guy but he still loved her. Fifty years from now he'd love her. Maybe one day he'd wax nostalgic to some young man about his first love, and it would seem better than it actually was.

But so what, Ben thought, and he kissed her. Jessica kissed him back. Cherry lip balm; he'd been wrong about the unscented lip gloss. She squeezed his arms. He pulled away and she took a breath, looking up at him. The youngest girl he'd ever seen, pretending just like him.

"Honey, one hundred years ago you'd break my heart," Ben said. He pushed her gently into the hall and shut the door.

He stood in the middle of his living room and waited until he heard her footsteps echoing down the stairs, then the slam of a car door and the roar of an engine. He grabbed the box and pulled out the newspaper.

At the bottom lay a gold lion's head belt buckle.

"So you never saw Ginger again?" Patrick waved his arms. "That was *it*?"

Ben missed his layup. He let the ball bounce and roll across the court. They played in a park across the street from his apartment, with netless rims and a chain-link fence that sliced the sun into yellow diamonds. He'd been gone a little more than a week but it was already mid-summer hot, that smell of warm pavement and exhaust.

"That was it," Ben said. "I thought she might have run back to her pimp, so I stopped by on my way home, to the bus stop where we first picked her up. You know what I found? Another hooker."

Patrick laughed. "You should've brought her back. I'd fuck a hooker."

"How hot was Ginger?" Steve asked.

"Pretty hot," Ben said.

"Scale of one to ten. One being Jim's mom, ten being that hostess at Applebee's."

"The hostess at Jack Astor's," Jim said.

Steve waved him off. "Don't be a douche bag. The Applebee's hostess is more . . . what's the word I'm looking for."

"Fuckable," Ben said.

"We're not rating fuckable," Jim said. "We're rating hot."

Steve frowned. "Same thing."

"It's not," Patrick said. "Ben's ex Jessica is hotter than Samantha, but I'd much rather fuck Samantha. No offense, Ben."

"None taken."

"Whatever," Steve said. "I want to know about Ginger. Come on, Ben. One to ten."

"Are we still talking about fuckability?"

"Jesus, who cares?" Steve retrieved the ball. "Just give us a rating."

"Eight," Ben said.

"Awesome," Steve said, and Jim and Patrick jockeyed for position under the hoop as Steve launched a shot. Ben stared past them, toward the boulevard with its traffic and horizon of low-slung strip malls and plazas. The air smelled like plastic again. This time, Ben knew what it was.

On the way home from the basketball court he stopped at the old man's house. The lawn was brown from drought and leaves had collected on the steps. Ben pounded on the door and called for the old man but only heard the echoes of his fist. He walked around the back and peered through the windows; he saw a living room with furniture and little else—the stacks of books and papers he'd seen that morning when the old man answered the door with a muffin in one hand and an electric razor in the other were gone. Some dishes sat on the kitchen counter. A recycling bin filled with plastic Coke bottles waited on the linoleum floor.

Ben tried the garage door and it squeaked open. Late-day summer sun washed over the dusty cement floor. A push broom leaned against the wall, next to a bag of mulch and a garden spade with dried dirt pasted to its blade. The cherry red 1958 Ford Fairlane Skyliner was gone. In its place, an outline.

"I would have given you the Lincoln," Ben said aloud. "That son of a bitch didn't even have an engine."

Broome was how he remembered. Quiet and flat, with subdivisions marked by power lines and sound-deflecting fences erected along the highway. His childhood home was a modest ranch with seasonal decorations on the front door; in the winter a wreath, in the fall an inflated vinyl skeleton, and now, in the summer, a plastic penguin wiping sweat from its forehead.

Ben took the key from its usual spot underneath the second piece of slate and rummaged through the front closet until he found his father's blue-and-white sneakers. He stared at them for a moment, brushed some of the crusted dirt off the stiff laces, and scratched clean the blue Nike swoosh. Then he stuffed them into the kitchen garbage, tied the bag shut, and brought it out to the cans standing near the garage. He watched TV on the couch until his mom came home late from work.

She took off her shoes and sat next to him. Her gray suit looked worn. She undid her hair. "Ben, is that your car?"

"Uh-huh."

"It's nice. Was it expensive?"

"Not really. I bought it used."

"It looks expensive, though. Do you need any money?"

"I'm okay. I sold some stuff."

"What kind of stuff?"

"An Elvis belt buckle."

She yawned. "Oh, well, that explains it. People go crazy for Elvis. I never understood the appeal." She put her hand on his shoulder. "Are you staying for dinner?"

"Of course."

"You know, Jessica called a few days ago. She said you weren't answering your cell phone."

"I saw her."

"And are you two getting back together?"

Ben smiled and shook his head.

"Thank God," his mom said. "You know I never cared for that girl. Too fickle."

18.

*B*en leaned back with his cell pressed to one ear. He watched the dying sun glint off the water. He listened to the wind and the sounds of people walking below.

"Is this Alex?"

His apartment was clean and spare with a small patio for watching the sun set. He'd bought a canvas and a beginner's oil painting set but they sat in his room, unopened. Instead he filled his days with wandering. A Dutch language class; a hash bar with bad paintings on the wall; a canal cruise with some fat Americans; a nightclub where he'd met a German girl and they fooled around in the backseat of her car.

"Who's this?"

"Ben. Ben Fish. Do you remember—"

"Coyote Café. You and Elvis. Of course I remember. That was like a month ago."

"Thirty-three days."

"You've been counting?"

"Yep."

Ben was a little surprised there'd been no dramatic transformation, no epiphanies. Just some mild culture shock—he was embarrassed to speak only one language after meeting a Dutch couple who spoke fluent English, German, and French—and the occasional lonely morning, because he'd always felt mornings were lonelier than nights.

"How was Memphis?" Ben said.

"Okay, I guess. Fiona hooked up with a guy in his forties and Heather and I saw a terrible Elvis band. The singer didn't look anything like him. Not as bad as your grandpa, though."

"He wasn't my grandpa."

"Oh, that's right. I forgot. It's been thirty-three days, you know."

One afternoon Ben swore he spotted the old man walking past a fountain in the Rijksmuseum Gardens. He ran to catch up with him and saw it was a middle-aged tourist in a white jumpsuit with shiny black boots and thick gold-rimmed aviator sunglasses. Eating popcorn from a paper bag, street map in hand, reading over the top of his sunglasses.

"So," Alex said. "Did Elvis ever find his granddaughter?"

"He did."

"Reconciliation, I hope."

"Not quite."

A few days earlier in the top floor of an English bookstore Ben heard the cashier singing "Suspicious Minds," and he expected the old man to walk out of the back room, carrying a stack of books, a trail of employees following close behind. On one of the racks sat a gossip rag, the front page a grainy doctored photo of an old fat man in a white jumpsuit exiting a classic car—maybe a 1958 Ford Fairlane Skyliner, Ben couldn't be sure—with a younger woman wearing sunglasses. The headline read:

ELVIS CONTACTS DAUGHTER
SHOCKING DETAILS OF THEIR
TEARFUL REUNION

"Don't you think this is a little weird?" Alex said. "I mean, I'm not trying to ruin the reunion vibe, but it's been over a month—"

"I had to make some arrangements. Is that a bad excuse?"

"It's a terrible excuse."

"Well, I wanted to let you know that you were right. The Kit Kats are better here."

Silence. Alex laughed. Then she laughed some more.

They talked while Ben watched the sun set over the Herengracht Canal. The canals weren't as big as he thought they'd be, little rivers running along city streets with canal boats that looked silly because it seemed so much easier to walk or bike. But sometimes he didn't want to walk or bike. Sometimes he wanted to get on one of those canal boats and pretend he was headed for parts unknown, to the edge of the map, all the way to the end of the universe and through the keyhole in God's bathroom door. To a place bigger than his father. Bigger than the world. Bigger than anything he ever knew.

ACKNOWLEDGMENTS

Born during lunch in the backyard of a Cambridge home—DG laughed the longest and hardest at the karaoke scene. I'm indebted to the incomparable Jud Laghi, and to Sarah Self, who pushed when it needed pushing. Steve Trefonides and Brian Jenkins read the early drafts and offered much-needed feedback. Heather Lazare provided better edits than anything I could have come up with. Peter Guralnick's Elvis bios were an invaluable resource. Jake Halpern was a mensch, as always. Ted Wyman offered his Back Bay apartment as a rock-and-roll sanctuary. Leslie Esptein and Ha Jin filled in the gaps.

Mom, Dad, Sis—gratitude would take up too much space and reader patience. This is yours. It always was. Anything good in these pages is the result of my wife's encouragement, her careful eyes, and her uncanny ability to get me back to the shed.

ABOUT THE AUTHOR

Micah Nathan is an award-winning author, screenwriter, and essayist. His debut novel, *Gods of Aberdeen*, became an international bestseller.

Nathan's short stories have been a finalist for the Tobias Wolff Award for Short Fiction and the Innovative Fiction Award, and his work has appeared in the *Gettysburg Review*, the *Bellingham Review*, *Boston Globe Magazine*, *Eclectica*, *Diagram*, *Glimmer Train*, and other national publications. He received his MFA from Boston University, where he was awarded the 2010 Saul Bellow Prize in Fiction. He currently lives in the Boston area with his wife, their dog, and an assortment of curiosities.